"十三五"国家重点出版规划项目

李白诗歌全集英译
A Complete Edition of Pai Li's Poems in Chinese and English
With Annotations

赵彦春　译·注
Translated and Annotated by Yanchun Chao

第二卷
Volume Ⅱ

上海大学出版社
·上海·

卷二

目 录
Contents

277 乐府四十四首
Conservatoire, 44 Poems

279 门有车马客行
Carts and Steeds at the Gate

282 君子有所思行
A Gentleman in Thought

285 东海有勇妇
A Brave Woman at East Sea

289 黄葛篇
The Gold Vine

291 白马篇
The White Horse

294 凤笙篇
The Phoenix and Flute

296 怨歌行
A Sad Song

298 塞下曲六首
A Border Song, Six Poems

309 来日大难
A Hard Day

312 塞上曲
A Border Tune

314 玉阶怨
Complaint of the Jade Steps

315	襄阳曲四首
	A Sowshine Tune, Four Poems
319	大堤曲
	The Dike
320	宫中行乐词八首
	Playing in the Palace, Eight Poems
330	清平调词三首
	Pure Peace Tune, Three Poems
333	鼓吹入朝曲
	Attending Levee in Music
335	秦女休行
	The Ch'in Belle Is Pardoned
337	秦女卷衣
	The Ch'in Belle Prepares His Array
339	东武吟
	Ode to Eastmight
342	邯郸才人嫁为厮养卒妇
	A Beauty from Hantan Married to a Servant
344	出自蓟北门行
	Out of the North Gate of Chi
347	洛阳陌
	On the Thoroughfare in Loshine
348	北上行
	Going Up North
351	短歌行
	A Short Song
353	空城雀
	Sparrows o'er the Town
355	菩萨蛮
	Bodhisattva Bun
356	忆秦娥
	Missing Fair Ch'in

359		乐府三十八首 Conservatoire, 38 Poems
361		发白马 Starting from Whitehorse Ford
363		陌上桑 The Mulberry Gatherer
366		枯鱼过河泣 The Wounded Fish Cries
368		丁督护歌 The Song of Captain
370		相逢行 Seeing Her
373		千里思 Missing the One
375		树中草 Grass in the Woods
376		君马黄 Yellow，Steed Thine
378		拟古 In Ancient Style
380		折杨柳 Plucking a Willow Twig
381		少年子 A Youngster
382		紫骝马 The Brown Horse
383		少年行二首 The Young Man，Two Poems
386		白鼻䯄 White-nosed Brown Horse
387		豫章行 The Yüchang Hill

390	沐浴子	When Taking a Bath
391	高句骊	Koreans
392	静夜思	Night Thought
393	渌水曲	Blue Water
394	凤凰曲	A Phoenix Song
395	凤台曲	A Tune of Phoenix Mound
396	从军行	A War Poem
398	秋思	Longing in Autumn
400	春思	Longing in Spring
401	秋思	Longing in Autumn
403	子夜吴歌四首	Wu Tunes by a Girl Called Midnight, Four Poems
407	对酒行	Toasting
409	估客行	Leaving No Trail
410	捣衣篇	Pestling on Clothes
413	少年行	The Gallant Boy
416	长歌行	A Long Song Ballad

418	长相思	
	Long Longing	
420	猛虎行	
	Tiger Tune	
425	去妇词	
	A Deserted Wife	

431　古近体诗二十八首
Old-new Rhythmic Poetry, 28 Poems

433	襄阳歌	
	Song of Sowshine	
437	南都行	
	South Town	
440	江上吟	
	A Croon on the River	
442	侍从宜春苑奉诏赋龙池柳色初青听新莺百啭歌	
	Accompanying His Majesty in Fair Spring Park and Composing a Poem at His Request to Describe the Spring at Dragon Pool While Warblers Sing	
444	玉壶吟	
	A Song of the Jade Pot	
446	豳歌行上新平长史兄粲	
	A Pin Song, to My Cousin Ts'an, Vice Prefect	
449	西岳云台歌送丹丘子	
	A Song to Redknoll at Cloud Mound of Mt. Flora	
452	元丹丘歌	
	A Song to Redknoll	
454	扶风豪士歌	
	A Song of the Gallant	
457	同族弟金城尉叔卿烛照山水壁画歌	
	Looking at a Scroll with a Candle with My Cousin, a Constable	

459	白毫子歌	
	A Song of White Frills	
461	梁园吟	
	A Song of Liang's Garden	
465	鸣皋歌送岑徵君	
	A Song of Swamp to Ts'en the Recruit	
470	鸣皋歌奉饯从翁清归五崖山居	
	A Song of Swamp at a Farewell Dinner for Uncle Ch'ing Back to Mt. Five Cliffs	
472	劳劳亭歌	
	A Song of Farewell Bower	
474	横江词六首	
	The Heng River, Six Poems	
480	金陵城西楼月下吟	
	Crooning on Moonlit West Tower in Gold Hill Town	
482	东山吟	
	A Song of the East Hills	
484	僧伽歌	
	A Song of a Monk	
486	白云歌送刘十六归山	
	A Song of White Clouds to Liu Sixteen	
487	金陵歌送别范宣	
	A Song of the Gold Hills, Farewell to Hsuan Fan	
490	笑歌行	
	Laughing and Singing	
494	悲歌行	
	A Sad Song	

乐府四十四首
Conservatoire, 44 Poems

门有车马客行

门有车马宾,
金鞍耀朱轮。
谓从丹霄落,
乃是故乡亲。
呼儿扫中堂,
坐客论悲辛。
对酒两不饮,
停觞泪盈巾。
叹我万里游,
飘摇三十春。
空谈帝王略,
紫绶不挂身。
雄剑藏玉匣,
阴符生素尘。
廓落无所合,
流离湘水滨。
借问宗党间,
多为泉下人。
生苦百战役,
死托万古邻。
北风扬胡沙,
埋翳周与秦。
大运且如此,
苍穹宁匪仁?
恻怆竟何道,
存亡任大钧。

Carts and Steeds at the Gate

The gate sees carts, steeds and their zeal;
The gold saddle suits the red wheel.
He says he comes back from the crown,
Feeling close to the folks of the town.
I ask my son to sweep the hall,
So we'll talk about rise and fall.
Before we have finished our cup,
Our eyes warming with tears well up.
I've travelled three thousand miles now,
Against thirty years' rain and sough.
We've talked about grand plans in vain,
With no ribbons or ranks to gain.
My sharp sword in the cask does hide;
My martial books are left aside.
None agrees with me any more;
I tour the Hsiang and stroll ashore.
Of those who understand me well
Most fare badly down in the hell.
On earth a hundred wars we've fought;
In hell ten thousand mates we've got.
A wind whirls up in northern land;
Chough and Ch'in are buried in sand.
Heaven has everything arranged;
How can our worldly life be changed?
So sad, what can we say but sigh?
To live or die, just rest on the sky.

* the Hsiang: the most important river in today's Hunan Province.
* Chough: Chough (1046 B.C.- 256 B.C.), the regime established after Shang perished, the last slavery society in China. There were two periods in the Chough dynasty, Western Chough (1046 B.C.- 771 B.C.) and Eastern Chough (770 B.C.- 256 B.C.). Eastern Chough consists of two periods: the Spring and Autumn period and the Warring States period.
* Ch'in: Originally, Ch'in was a state that was a good help to the Kingdom of Shang against western barbarians. In 905 B.C. during King Piety of Chough's reign, it was enfeoffed as a dependency of Chough. In 770 B.C., appreciated by King Peace of Chough for its act of protecting Chough, it was formally recognized as a vassal state of Chough. In 221 B.C., after exterminating other states it became a great empire, i.e., the Ch'in Empire.
* Heaven: the space surrounding or seeming to overarch the earth, in which the sun, the moon, and stars appear, popularly the abode of God, his angels and the blessed, and in most cases suggesting supernatural power or sometimes signifying a monarch.

君子有所思行

紫阁连终南，
青冥天倪色。
凭崖望咸阳，
宫阙罗北极。
万井惊画出，
九衢如弦直。
渭水银河清，
横天流不息。
朝野盛文物，
衣冠何翕赩。
厩马散连山，
军容威绝域。
伊皋运元化，
卫霍输筋力。
歌钟乐未休，
荣去老还逼。
圆光过满缺，
太阳移中昃。
不散东海金，
何争西飞匿。
无作牛山悲，
恻怆泪沾臆。

A Gentleman in Thought

The court with Mt. South End does link;

The skyline o'er there looks like ink.
Uphill I gaze at Allshine far;
The palaces link with Pole Star.
The broad ways crisscross as if drawn;
The thoroughfares stretch straightly on.
The Wei River's like silver bright,
Flowing forward till out of sight.
The court's rules are all well run;
Bright robes and caps the courtiers don.
Stables by the mountains disperse;
The troops o'erpower the universe.
Talents like Yin and Potter aid;
Fighters like Wei and Swift Huo raid.
Bells and lutes are going on there;
No longer young, I have gray hair.
The moon that waxes will soon wane;
The sun that's high won't there remain.
At high noon I did not give all;
Why should I vie? Night will soon fall.
Before Mt. Bull one should not cry;
Over our tears, we should not sigh.

* Mt. South End: one of the main peaks of the Ch'in Ridge Mountains, and Purple is a peak of Mt. South End. Mt. South End also stands for the South Hills, also known as the Southern Mountains, Mt. Great One, Mt. Earthlungs, the mountains south of Long Peace, a great stronghold of the capital, towering in the middle of Ch'in Ridge and rolling about 100 kilometers. It is the birthplace of Wordist culture, Buddhist culture, Filial Piety culture, Longevity culture, Bellheads culture and Plutus culture and is praised as the Capital of Fairies, the crown of Heavenly Abode and the Promised Land of the World.
* Pole Star: indicating the place where emperors dwell.
* the Wei River: the largest branch of the Yellow River, originating from today's Mt.

Birdmouse in Kansu Province, flowing through Precious Rooster, Allshine, Long Peace, and meeting the Yellow River at T'ung Pass.

* Yin: referring to Yin Ee (1649 B.C.- 1549 B.C.), a renowned statesman, thinker and one of the earliest known Wordist. In his term as a prime minister, he led Shang to become an economically and politically flourishing society through rectifying the bureaucracy and taking measures to improve the livelihood of the people.
* Potter: Moor Potter (cir. 2219 B.C.- 2113 B.C.), a great statesman, thinker, and educator of the ancient times, recognized as the originator of Chinese judicature by historians and regarded as one of the Four Sages of ancient times, along with Mound, Hibiscus and Worm.
* Wei: referring to Ch'ing Wei (? - 106 B.C.), an outstanding general against the Huns in the Han dynasty. As a commander, he was strict about orders but caring for his soldiers; as an official, he was polite and generous to his colleagues even in a high-ranking position.
* Huo: referring to Swift Huo (140 B.C.- 117 B.C.), a renowned general, prominent strategist and patriotic hero in the Han dynasty. He made his first show at 17, leading 800 fierce cavalrymen to penetrate into enemy lines and defeat the Huns. Huo fought against the Huns in three major wars and returned with victory each time. He died of illness at 24, leaving his achievements as one of the highest glory for Chinese military commanders.
* Mt. Bull: Lord Scene of Ch'i once wept at the sight of the landscape on Mt. Bull, sinking into deep melancholy of mortality.

东海有勇妇

梁山感杞妻,
恸哭为之倾。
金石忽暂开,
都由激深情。
东海有勇妇,
何惭苏子卿。
学剑越处子,
超然若流星。
损躯报夫仇,
万死不顾生。
白刃耀素雪,
苍天感精诚。
十步两躩跃,
三呼一交兵。
斩首掉国门,
蹴踏五藏行。
豁此伉俪愤,
粲然大义明。
北海李使君,
飞章奏天庭。
舍罪警风俗,
流芳播沧瀛。
名在列女籍,
竹帛已光荣。
淳于免诏狱,
汉主为缇萦。
津妾一棹歌,

脱父于严刑。
十子若不肖，
不如一女英。
豫让斩空衣，
有心竟无成。
要离杀庆忌，
壮夫所素轻。
妻子亦何辜，
焚之买虚声。
岂如东海妇，
事立独扬名。

A Brave Woman at East Sea

The Beam Mountains so moved did fall
For Fruit Beam's wife and for her squall.
Even metals and rocks may move
For someone's pathos and deep love.
A brave woman there at East Sea,
Better than Tsuching Su she could be.
Swordplay from a Yüeh maid she learned;
Fast she leaped and swiftly she turned.
To revenge his wrong as a wife,
She fought regardless of her life.
Her blade so swayed did like snow shine;
The Heaven was moved by her whine.
She paced on and leaped to and fro,
And charged with three shouts and one blow.
She cut off the enemy's pate,
And hung it high on the tower gate.

She stamped on his bowels with passion;
So praised was her indignation.
Sir Li from North Sea did report
Her brave act to the Lord at court.
A pardon was given thereby,
And her story spread far and nigh.
Now her name has been carved with pride;
The glory exceeds time and tide.
Ch'un Yü was free from penalty
Thanks to his daughter's bravery.
A ferry girl sang a boat song,
And thus revenged her father's wrong.
Ten sons, if nothing they can do,
Cannot match a woman flower true.
Yüjang just cut off Chao's array;
He had the will but not the way.
Yaolee failed to kill in his fight,
Hence incurring all brave men's slight.
E'en his wife and sons did complain,
And burned him to wash off the stain.
How can they with this wife compare?
Her act lets her fame last for e'er.

* the Beam Mountains: in Southwest Lu, that is, the southwest part of today's Shantung Province.
* East Sea: what is known as East China Sea today.
* Fruit Beam: a senior official of Ch'i, who died in a fierce battle. It is said that his wife cried for his death for ten days, which was so moving that even the wall fell for her wail.
* Tsuching Su: a virtuous girl who took revenge for her father in her 20s.
* a Yüeh maid: referring to the Yüeh girl who was good at swordplay and once had a fight with White Ape.

* Sir Li: also known as North Sea Li because he was once prefect of North Sea, a famous official, poet and calligrapher in the T'ang dynasty, Pai Li and Fu Tu's friend.
* North Sea: a shire or prefecture in the T'ang dynasty, what is Ch'ingchow in today's Shantung Province. Sir Li was the prefecture chief of North Sea.
* Ch'unyü: an official in the Han dynasty who had five daughters but no son. He was once sentenced to penalty. When he was transferred to the capital, his youngest daughter went along with him, and asked the emperor for pardon by voluntarily registering as a servant in the palace. The emperor was moved by her sincerity, so he exempted Ch'unyü from punishment.
* A ferry girl: Lord Chao was about to attack the State of Ch'u, but the ferry official, heavily drunk, missed the time. The daughter of the official entreated the lord not to kill her father until he was sober, and ferried the men across the river. When they paddled in the middle of the river, the ferry girl started singing a song to excuse her father and make wishes to the lord. The lord was moved and released her father.
* Yüjang: an assassin who wanted to take revenge for his master by killing Hsiangtsu Chao. He was captured after three failures. Knowing there would be no chance anymore, he asked Chao to let him stab his robe as if he had completed his mission. Chao agreed, and the assassin cut himself after he finished three stabs on his robe.
* Yaolee: an assassin in the State of Wu. To complete his mission, he asked his lord to kill his wife in order to win the target's trust. As he finally had the chance to kill his target, he failed in the fight and found it was not a noble mission, so he committed suicide.

黄　葛　篇

黄葛生洛溪，
黄花自绵幂。
青烟万条长，
缭绕几百尺。
闺人费素手，
采缉作絺绤。
缝为绝国衣，
远寄日南客。
苍梧大火落，
暑服莫轻掷。
此物虽过时，
是妾手中迹。

The Gold Vine

The gold vine sprawls by the Lo Stream;
With dense leaves the yellow flowers beam.
The mist over ten thousand vines,
And hundreds of feet it entwines.
A woman picks vines with hands fair,
Wherewith gold vine cloth she'll prepare.
She will sew clothing for her man
So guard the State's border he can.
In Green Wood, Fire has gone away,
But don't leave aside your array.
Although gone out of season now,

It's from your wife, with love enow.

* gold vine: a kind of kudzu vine, the fibre of which can be processed from its stems or barks into the material for cloth or paper.
* the Lo Stream: unidentified in this poem.
* Green Wood: Ts'angwu if transliterated, a shire established during the reign of Emperor Martial of Han, which is now Wuchow.
* Fire: referring to a star which indicates season change in ancient Chinese astrology. When it appears in due south at dawn, coldness declines; when it appears in due south at night, heat declines.

白　马　篇

龙马花雪毛，
金鞍五陵豪。
秋霜切玉剑，
落日明珠袍。
斗鸡事万乘，
轩盖一何高。
弓摧南山虎，
手接太行猱。
酒后竞风采，
三杯弄宝刀。
杀人如剪草，
剧孟同游遨。
发愤去函谷，
从军向临洮。
叱咤经百战，
匈奴尽奔逃。
归来使酒气，
未肯拜萧曹。
羞入原宪室，
荒淫隐蓬蒿。

The White Horse

A snow-white dragon horse you ride；
The saddle gold，you beam with pride.
Your sharpened sword does hoarfrost don；

Your pearled robe lures the setting sun.
With cockfighting you serve the Lord;
What a high-crest cart you now board!
You kill a tiger with your arm;
You catch a monkey with your palm.
You go high after drinking wine;
With your cup you greet your blade shine.
You kill people like cutting grass,
But Chümeng can be of your class.
To Case Dale Pass you start to go;
In Lint'ao there you'll fight the foe.
With hails, you've fought many a fight;
The Huns are put to pell-mell flight.
You still drink, back from battlefield,
Unwilling to Hsiao and Ts'ao yield.
You feel shame to live like Yüanhsien,
Living in wormwood, a poor man.

* tiger: a large carnivorous mammal of the cat family, which originated in Asia, with vertical black wavy stripes on a tawny body and black bars or rings on the limbs and tail, praised as king of all animals.
* cockfighting: referring to the game of cockfight. Cockfighting has a long history in China, a main recreational activity all through history. The earliest cockfighting in China recorded in *Historical Records* was in 770 B.C.
* Chümeng: a knight in the Fore-Ch'in period, who often saved people from danger.
* Case Dale Pass: an ancient pass located to the east of Long Peace, the capital of the T'ang Empire, and Lint'ao, a noted county was to the west.
* Lint'ao: Lint'ao County under today's Settled West (Tinghsi), Kansu Province, one of the sources of the Yellow River culture, instituted as a county in 384 B.C. though with a different name and changed to the present name in 1929. It is entitled as Town of Poetry, Town of Horticulture, Town of Flowers and so on.
* Hun: war-like nomadic peoples occupying vast regions from Mongolia to Central Asia in Chinese history, especially during the Han dynasty. They were a constant menace on

China's western and northern borders.
* Hsiao: referring to Ho Hsiao (257 B.C.- 193 B.C.), a statesman, prime minister and one of the founding fathers of Han.
* Ts'ao: referring to Ts'an Ts'ao (? -190 B.C.), the second prime minister of Han after Ho Hsiao.
* Yüanhsien: a disciple of Confucius. Although he lived in poverty, he stayed calm, playing string music and singing.

凤笙篇

仙人十五爱吹笙，
学得昆丘彩凤鸣。
始闻炼气餐金液，
复道朝天赴玉京。
玉京迢迢几千里，
凤笙去去无穷已。
欲叹离声发绛唇，
更嗟别调流纤指。
此时惜别讵堪闻，
此地相看未忍分。
重吟真曲和清吹，
却奏仙歌响绿云。
绿云紫气向函关，
访道应寻緱氏山。
莫学吹笙王子晋，
一遇浮丘断不还。

The Phoenix and Flute

The sprite likes to play the flute at fifteen,
Like a phoenix uphill trills to sheen.
I hear he refines air for nectar gold,
And you're to pay respect to Lord, I'm told.
The capital's a thousand miles away,
And with your flute stay there for aye you may.
Sigh upon sigh issues from your red lips;

And parting tune flows from your finger tips.
Now this parting tune I can't tolerate,
And to part from you at this place I hate.
A clear tune I sing to the flute you blow,
And you play a fairy song to the blue.
Green clouds and Purple Air to Dale Pass glow,
To seek the Word, to Mt. Kou I should go.
You should not learn from the flute blowing prince,
Who met Float Knoll and has there stayed e'er since.

* flute: a tubular wind instrument of small diameter with holes along the side.
* the sprite: referring to Prince of Front, a son of King Spirit of Chough, who had been intelligent and courageous since childhood. Though he was Crown Prince, he had few desires and was keen on the Word. In some legends, he knew his mortality and became immortal.
* refine air: a way for the ancients to exercise inner essence through regulating breath and driving inner air.
* nectar gold: a kind of elixir.
* green clouds: auspicious clouds flowing around immortals.
* Purple Air: In Chinese astrology, it is a star near Jupiter, which is regarded as an auspicious sign.
* Dale Pass: Case Dale Pass, an ancient pass located to the east of T'ang's capital.
* the Word: referring to Tao if transliterated, the most significant and profoundest concept in Chinese philosophy. According to Laocius's *The Word and the World*: "The Word is void, but its use is infinite. O deep! It seems to be the root of all things."
* Mt. Kou: where Prince of Front became immortal.
* Float Knoll: an immortal, used to travel in Mt. Tower with Prince of Front.

怨　歌　行

十五入汉宫，
花颜笑春红。
君王选玉色，
侍寝金屏中。
荐枕娇夕月，
卷衣恋春风。
宁知赵飞燕，
夺宠恨无穷。
沉忧能伤人，
绿鬓成霜蓬。
一朝不得意，
世事徒为空。
鹔鹴换美酒，
舞衣罢雕龙。
寒苦不忍言，
为君奏丝桐。
肠断弦亦绝，
悲心夜忡忡。

A Sad Song

She's chosen for Lord at fifteen;
Flowers bloom with her giggle between.
The Lord likes the color of jade
That serves Him behind a gold shade.
Her pillow makes the moon feel shy;

Her sleeve rolled to the wind clings nigh.
Flying Swallow's come here to pose;
She has all His favor, my woes.
Gloom all day can a person blight;
Black sideburns will become frost white.
Once you have failed to have your day,
The world so void, nothing will stay.
Sell the kingfisher for good wine;
Sway your dress of dragons benign.
The hardship is too much to tell;
Let me for your sake strike the bell.
The bell breaks up due to my plight;
I'm sad and sadder night by night.

* she: referring to Lady Pan (48 B.C.- A.D. 2), an imperial concubine. Her life from being coveted to being disgraced implies the poet's frustration in his unappreciated career.
* Flying Swallow: referring to Feiyan Chao (45 B.C.- 1 B.C.). Starting as a dancer in the residence of Princess Yang'o, she attracted Emperor Complete of Han's attention, hence she was made an imperial concubine of the highest rank and then crowned as empress. It is said that she was of so slight a build that she could dance on the palm of a hand.
* wine: one of the most important beverages in Chinese culture, of which brown wine was brewed more than three thousand years ago and white wine (spirit) became popular in the Sung dynasty. Wine has an important position in Chinese life, such as literary creation, cultural activities, health care, cookery and so on.

塞下曲六首

A Border Song, Six Poems

其 一

五月天山雪，
无花只有寒。
笛中闻折柳，
春色未曾看。
晓战随金鼓，
宵眠抱玉鞍。
愿将腰下剑，
直为斩楼兰。

No. 1

The fifth moon Mt. Heaven's all snow;
Only coldness, no blossoms blow.
From the flute a pluck-willow lay,
We cannot yet see a spring day.
The drum beaten, to war we leap;
Saddle in arms, we're half asleep.
I'll take off my sword from my waist,
To kill all Hun foes with brows raised.

* Mt. Heaven: one of the seven mountain chains in the world, 2,500 kilometers long, 250 to 350 kilometers wide on average.
* flute: a tubular wind instrument of small diameter with holes along the side.
* Hun: one of barbaric nomadic Asian peoples who frequently invaded China, a general term referring to all northern or western invaders.

* Lowland: Kroraina, a small city-state in the western regions, specifically in the western border of the basin of Lop Nor, having an important position on the Silk Road, which was founded in 176 B.C. and mysteriously disappeared in A.D. 630.

其 二

天兵下北荒，
胡马欲南饮。
横戈从百战，
直为衔恩甚。
握雪海上餐，
拂沙陇头寝。
何当破月氏，
然后方高枕。

No. 2

Our Heavenly troops north wilds raid,
As Hun horses South Land invade.
Spears as pillows, we've fought as such,
Because His favor we've had much.
On the desert eat snow we could;
At Mt. Bulge sleep in sand we would.
When can we the Hun foes destroy,
And henceforth a sound sleep enjoy?

* Hun: referring to nomadic nationalities north and west of China, who had no trade but battle and carnage, no fields or plough lands but only wastes where white bones lay scattered over yellow sands.
* South Land: referring to T'ang in contrast with northern and western areas where barbarians lived.
* Mt. Bulge: a mountain located in the southeast of present-day Kansu Province, 2,928 meters above sea level and about 240 kilometers long from north to south, the borderline between Sha'anhsi Loess Plateau and West Bulge Loess Plateau.

其 三

骏马似风飙,
鸣鞭出渭桥。
弯弓辞汉月,
插羽破天骄。
阵解星芒尽,
营空海雾消。
功成画麟阁,
独有霍嫖姚。

No. 3

The fine horse flies like a wind blows;
One whip at Wei Bridge, here it goes.
We go ahead arrow and bow;
To fight the Huns, to kill the foe.
Battle over, no starlight rays;
Barracks empty, no desert haze.
Only General Swift Huo alone
Was awarded and got well known.

* horse: a large herbivorous solid-hoofed quadruped (*Equus caballus*) with coarse mane and tail, of various strains: Ferghana, Mongolian, Kazaks, Hequ, Karasahr and so on and of various colors: black, white, yellow, brown, dappled and so on, domesticated about four thousand years go, reared as a pet, employed as a beast of draught and burden and especially for riding upon. Horses have played an important part in human civilization, widely employed in agriculture, transportation and warefare.
* Hun: one of barbaric nomadic Asian peoples who frequently invaded China, a general term referring to all northern or western invaders.
* Swift Huo: Swift Huo (140 B.C.- 117 B.C.), a renowned general, prominent strategist

and patriotic hero in the Han dynasty. He made his first show at 17, leading 800 fierce cavalrymen to penetrate into enemy lines and defeat the Huns. Huo fought against the Huns in three major wars and each time returned with victory. He died of illness at 24, leaving his achievements as one of the highest glories for Chinese military commanders.

其 四

白马黄金塞，
云砂绕梦思。
那堪愁苦节，
远忆边城儿。
萤飞秋窗满，
月度霜闺迟。
摧残梧桐叶，
萧飒沙棠枝。
无时独不见，
流泪空自知。

No. 4

White horses, barracks on the sand,
And pebbles all my dreams command.
This hardship one can hardly bear;
You're on the border far off there.
Fireflies bump against my window;
Moonlight lingers on my sorrow.
The parasol tree's blown to bow;
The cherry branches brave the sough.
Why Not Come Back I often croon;
My tears are but to myself known.

* firefly: any of a family (*Lampyridae*) of winged beetles, active at night, whose abdomens usually glow with a luminescent light.
* parasol tree: Chinese parasol tree (*Firmiana simplex*), tree of the hibiscus family native to Asia, growing as tall as 12 metres, having deciduous leaves and small greenish

white flowers that are borne in clusters.
* cherry: any of various trees (genus *Prunus*) of the rose family, related to the plum and the peach and bearing small, round or heart-shaped drupes enclosing a smooth pit; especially the sweet cherry, the sour cherry and the wild black cherry.
* *Why Not Come Back*: a poem composed by Ch'üanch'i Shen, a T'ang poet, about a wife's crooning of her husband who was guarding the frontier.

其 五

塞虏乘秋下，
天兵出汉家。
将军分虎竹，
战士卧龙沙。
边月随弓影，
胡霜拂剑花。
玉关殊未入，
少妇莫长嗟。

No. 5

In autumn, Huns launch an attack;
The Han troops will fight the foes back.
The court gives the order to sweep;
At night the troops will on sand sleep.
The border moon shines to the bow;
The Hun frost tints the sword to glow.
The soldiers have not reached Jade Gate;
Oh, wives, do not complain till late.

* Hun: one of barbaric nomadic Asian peoples who frequently invaded China, a general term referring to all northern or western invaders.
* Han: China or Chinese, a metonymy adopted because of the powerful Han Empire founded by Pang Liu, King of Han before he won the war and reunified China.
* the moon: the planet of the earth, which appears at night and gives off shining silvery light, an image of purity and solitude in Chinese culture.
* Jade Gate: Jade Gate Pass, an important military fort and passage on the Silk Road, built in the Han dynasty, located in the north of today's Tunhuang, Kansu Province. As is recorded, to guard against Hun invasions, Emperor Martial of Han formed

alliance with nations in the western regions to initiate the route between east and west, and instituted four sires and built two passes with beacons west of the Yellow River. Fortresses were made from Lingchü to Wine Spring in 111 B.C. and more fortresses made from Wine Spring to Jade Gate.

其 六

烽火动沙漠,
连照甘泉云。
汉皇按剑起,
还召李将军。
兵气天上合,
鼓声陇底闻。
横行负勇气,
一战净妖氛。

No. 6

The beacon o'er the desert ablaze
O'er Sweet Spring drives away the haze.
The Han Lord stands up, sword in hand,
And General Li's called to command.
The soldiers' shouts the blue sky shake;
The war drums down there Mt. Bulge quake.
Bravery with high spirits goes;
One fight finishes all those foes.

* beacon: a prominent building set on a wall or hill or a similar position, as a guide or warning to garrison generals or others.
* Sweet Spring: Sweet Spring Palace built by Emperor First on a mountain called Sweet Spring in Sha'anhsi Province.
* the Han Lord: referring to Lord Martial of Han (156 B.C.- 87 B.C.), the seventh emperor of the Han dynasty, a prominent statesman, strategist and poet, who made the empire prosperous in all aspects.
* General Li: Broad Li (? - 119 B.C.) in full name, Kuang Li if transliterated, a renowned general who won many battles against the Huns in the Han dynasty. Two of

his descendants left deep footprints in Chinese history, Hao Li (A.D. 351 – A.D. 417), King Martial Glare of West Cool (A.D. 400 – A.D. 421), and Yüan Li (A.D. 566 – A.D. 635), the founder and first emperor of T'ang.

* Mt. Bulge: a mountain located in the southeast of present-day Kansu Province, 2,928 meters above sea level and about 240 kilometers long from north to south, the borderline between Sha'anhsi Loess Plateau and West Bulge Loess Plateau.

来 日 大 难

来日一身，
携粮负薪。
道长食尽，
苦口焦唇。
今日醉饱，
乐过千春。
仙人相存，
诱我远学。
海凌三山，
陆憩五岳。
乘龙天飞，
目瞻两角。
授以神药，
金丹满握。
蟪蛄蒙恩，
深愧短促。
思填东海，
强衔一木。
道重天地，
轩师广成。
蝉翼九五，
以求长生。
下士大笑，
如苍蝇声。

A Hard Day

Life is hard to sustain;
We need firewood and grain.
The way is worse and worst;
We bear hunger and thirst.
If we're full with good cheer,
It's the best we hold dear.
A recluse with concern
Asks me to the Word learn.
O'er Three Hills I fly higher;
To Five Mounts I retire.
A dragon I ride, free;
Its two horns I can see.
I'm given nectar gold,
And elixir I hold.
Mole crickets have their way,
In this world a short stay.
With branches and twigs wee
Can Jayway fill the sea?
The Word holds sky and earth;
Lord Yellow learned Feat's worth.
E'en kingship we may spurn;
To long life we should turn.
A worldling may guffaw,
Like flies drone, just a bore.

* the Word: the Creator, the beginning of everything. It is identifiable with the Word or Logos in the West, as there is an enormous amount of common ground in the two

cosmologies and the doctrines concerning the most fundamental matters such as "the Word is the One" and "God is the One", and the personalization of Being, the progenitor of finite spirits, which are subordinate kinds of Beingor merely appearances of the Divine, the One.

* Three Hills: referring to the three fairy hills floating on East Sea.
* Five Mounts: the Five Mountains in China, including Mount Ever in Shanhsi, Mount Scale in Hunan, Mount Arch in Shantung, Mount Flora in Sha'anhsi, and Mount Tower in Honan, which symbolizes the unity of the Chinese nation from north, south, east, west and center.
* dragon: a fabulous serpent-like giant winged animal, a symbol of benevolence and sovereignty in Chinese culture.
* elixir: a hypothetical substance sought by medical alchemists to change base metals into gold or prolong life indefinitely.
* mole cricket: a burrowing cricket with a soft, cylindrical body and broad, mole-like front legs, found in some sandy soils.
* Jayway: According to legend, a daughter of Magic Farmer was drowned in East Sea and turned into a bird named Jayway. It looks like a crow or jay, but with an annular head, a white beak, and red feet, used to carrying stone and wood in an attempt to fill up the sea.
* Lord Yellow: alias Cartshaft, the first of the five heavenly gods in myth and the earliest ancestor of Chinese people. It was said that Lord Yellow made a tripod in the Chaste Hills. As the tripod was done, a dragon came down to visit him. He and his 70 or more officials and consorts all rode on the dragon and flew to the sky. In myth, when Lord Yellow and his retinue rode the dragon away, they left some junior officials on earth, who could but pull the dragon's beard in vain. All they got was only a strand of beard and the sword dropped from Lord Yellow.

塞 上 曲

大汉无中策，
匈奴犯渭桥。
五原秋草绿，
胡马一何骄。
命将征西极，
横行阴山侧。
燕支落汉家，
妇女无华色。
转战渡黄河，
休兵乐事多。
萧条清万里，
瀚海寂无波。

A Border Tune

The Han army has no way out;
The Huns have put Wei Bridge to rout.
The Five Plain's green with autumn grass;
The Hun horses leap high, alas.
The general's ordered to go west;
His troops run by Mt. Shade, hard pressed.
The Rouge Mountains are now occupied;
Hun women will lose their blonde pride.
By the Yellow there ends the fight;
In the ceasefire all take delight.
For three thousand miles rolls clear sand;

Without waves the great wilds expand.

* Han: China or Chinese, a metonymy adopted because of the powerful Han Empire founded by Pang Liu, King of Han before he won the war and reunified China.
* Hun: one of barbaric nomadic Asian peoples who frequently invaded China, a general term referring to all northern or western invaders.
* Five Plains: a shire established in the T'ang dynasty. According to historical records, the Huns garrisoned the north of the shire and used to harass the border.
* Mt. Shade: a range of mountains running from east to west, which is an important geographical watershed in North China.
* the Rouge Mountains: a range of mountains in Ope-arms, that is, today's Changyeh, Kansu Province, lush with pines and cypresses and various kinds of plants and grass.

玉 阶 怨

玉阶生白露，
夜久侵罗袜。
却下水晶帘，
玲珑望秋月。

Complaint of the Jade Steps

The jade steps there collect dew bright;
Her socks bear coldness in the night.
The crystal curtain she lets down;
The autumn moonlight does her drown.

* jade steps: the steps before, and leading to, a palace hall or a harem, usually built with marble, jade being a metaphor for good quality, often used as a metonymy for the court. A verse titled *Pear Blossoms in the Left Office* by another T'ang poet mentions the steps jade white, as reads: "The chill of theirs bullies the frost; / Their fragrance soaks into the night. / As spring wind blows, tossing and tossed, / They fly over the steps jade white."

襄阳曲四首
A Sowshine Tune, Four Poems

其 一

山公醉酒时，
酩酊高阳下。
头上白接䍦，
倒著还骑马。

No. 1

When Hillman reels about, so drunk,
The High Sun Pool seems to be sunk.
He wears a white cap propped aside,
The front back, on a horse astride.

* Sowshine: a famous historic city, about 2,800 years old, a birthplace of Ch'u, Han and Three Kingdom cultures, and a city of economic and military importance, in the northwest of present-day Hupei Province.
* Hillman: Chien Shan (A.D. 253 - A.D. 312), a celebrity and general in the Chin dynasty, the fifth son of T'ao Shan, one of the Seven Sages of the Bamboo Grove. He was as gentle and graceful as his father. When he was an official, the nation was falling apart and other officials were worried and depressed. Hillman, however, lived a casual life. When he hanged out, he used to hold a banquet and get drunk at the High Sun Pool.
* the High Sun Pool: a pool in Sowshine, a former pool to keep fish, owned by an official in the Han dynasty.

其 二

襄阳行乐处，
歌舞白铜鞮。
江城回绿水，
花月使人迷。

No. 2

Sowshine boasts a place for delight;
There's a song of *Leather Shoes White*.
Green water greens the river town;
In the moonlight all people drown.

---

* *Leather Shoes White*: a poem by Ning Hsu, a T'ang poet.

其 三

岘山临汉水，
水绿沙如雪。
上有堕泪碑，
青苔久磨灭。

No. 3

Mt. Steep sees the Han River flow,
The water green, the sand like snow.
Atop there's a tablet called Tear;
Worn out by moss, it looks unclear.

* Mt. Steep: an important fort in history, located in the southwest of Sowshine (Hsiangyang) with the Han River to its east.
* the Han River: the longest branch of the Long River, having an important position in Chinese history.
* a tablet called Tear: a tablet in memory of Lord Goat, a commander in the Chin dynasty, who garrisoned Sowshine. He promoted schooling and won over the trust of the people and the soldiers with nobility. To memorize his achievements, the people of Sowshine set a tablet on Mt. Steep. As the people couldn't help shedding tears once they saw the tablet, they named it Tablet Tear.
* moss: a tiny, delicate green bryophytic plant growing on damp decaying wood, wet ground, humid rocks or trees, producing capsules which open by an operculum and contain spores. Under a poet's writing brush, it may arouse a poetic feeling or imagination.

其 四

且醉习家池，
莫看堕泪碑。
山公欲上马，
笑杀襄阳儿。

No. 4

Drunk at Hsi's Pool, now very blear,
He's not going to Tablet Tear.
When Hillman's getting on the horse,
The children all laugh out with force.

* Hsi's Pool: an alternative name for the High Sun Pool, where Hillman used to have banquets.
* Tablet Tear: a tablet in memory of Lord Goat, a commander in the Chin dynasty, who garrisoned Sowshine.
* horse: a large herbivorous solid-hoofed quadruped (*Equus caballus*) with coarse mane and tail, domesticated about four thousand years go, reared as a pet, employed as a beast of draught and burden and especially for riding upon. Horses have played an important part in human civilization, widely employed in agriculture, transportation and warefare.

大 堤 曲

汉水临襄阳,
花开大堤暖。
佳期大堤下,
泪向南云满。
春风无复情,
吹我梦魂散。
不见眼中人,
天长音信断。

The Dike

The Han runs about Sowshine Town;
The flowers bloom and the dike is warm.
My love will come, all the way down;
Tears warming, I see south clouds swarm.
Loveless the spring wind seems to be;
It blows my soul off, now diffuse.
Where is my love now, where is she?
Heaven and earth turn on, no news!

* the Han River: the longest branch of the Long River, having an important position in Chinese history.
* Sowshine Town: Sowshine, a famous historic city, about 2,800 years old, a city of economic and military importance, in the northwest of present-day Hupei Province.
* Heaven: the space surrounding or seeming to overarch the earth, in which the sun, the moon, and stars appear, popularly the abode of God, his angels and the blessed, and in most cases suggesting supernatural power or sometimes signifying a monarch.

宫中行乐词八首
Playing in the Palace, Eight Poems

其 一

小小生金屋，
盈盈在紫微。
山花插宝髻，
石竹绣罗衣。
每出深宫里，
常随步辇归。
只愁歌舞散，
化作彩云飞。

No. 1

I was born in a golden house,
Now a dancer before the throne.
My topknot with orchids adorned,
And pink to my silk dress sewn.
I often follow Lord's sedan
In or out of the palace high.
I'm worried we may be dismissed,
Turning into hued clouds to fly.

* a golden house: referring to the palace Emperor Martial built for Petite, his cousin and love, now used as a metaphor for any palace or an abode for the fair sex.
* orchid: any of a widely distributed family of terrestrial or epiphytic monocotyledonous plants having thickened bulbous roots and often very showy distinctive flowers, one of the four most important floral images in Chinese literature, which are wintersweet, orchid, bamboo, and chrysanthemum.

其 二

柳色黄金嫩，
梨花白雪香。
玉楼巢翡翠，
金殿锁鸳鸯。
选妓随雕辇，
征歌出洞房。
宫中谁第一，
飞燕在昭阳。

No. 2

The willow puts on a gold hue;
Blossoms give off balm from the pear.
Upon the tower some halcyons nest;
Before the hall mandarin ducks pair.
Courtesans follow His sedan;
From the room flows a loving air.
In the harem who is the best?
Flying Swallow from Hall of Glare.

* willow: any of a large genus (*Salix*) of shrubs and trees related to the poplars, widely distributed in China and most of the world, having generally smooth branches, and often long, slender, pliant, and sometimes pendent branchlets, which seem to be waving good-bye, or weeping amorously, or drooping for nostalgia. It is a significant image in Chinese literature because of its litheness and charm.
* courtesans: professional women singers or lutenists, who were good at singing, dancing and traditional Chinese arts such as zither playing, go playing, calligraphy and painting.
* halcyon: a mythical bird, identified with the kingfisher, said to have nested on the sea

at the time of the winter solstice, when the sea was supposed to become calm.
* mandarin ducks: web-footed, short-legged, broad-billed water birds that always appear in loving pairs, a metaphor for couples in Chinese culture.
* Flying Swallow: referring to Feiyan Chao (45 B.C.–1 B.C.). Starting as a dancer in the residence of Princess Yang'o, a light as a swallow, she attracted Emperor Complete of Han's attention, hence she was appointed an imperial concubine and later crowned as empress.

其 三

卢橘为秦树，
蒲萄出汉宫。
烟花宜落日，
丝管醉春风。
笛奏龙吟水，
箫鸣凤下空。
君王多乐事，
还与万方同。

No. 3

In Han Palace entwine grape vines;
In High Park there grow orange trees.
Firecrackers suit the setting sun;
Bands and strings feel drunk in the breeze.
The flute sounds like dragons that drink;
The *hsow* breathes to phoenixes' coo.
His Majesty travels and plays,
Merging the world with his love true.

---

* Han Palace: a splendid imperial palace complex of Han, a metonymy for T'ang's palaces.
* grape: any grapevine yielding grapes, smooth skinned, edible, juicy, berrylike fruit, introduced to China by Chien Chang (164 B.C.- 114 B.C.) in the Han dynasty.
* orange: a reddish, yellow, round, edible citrus fruit, with a sweet, juicy pulp; any of various evergreen trees (genus *Citrus*) of the rue family bearing this fruit.
* High Park: an imperial park that Lord Martial of Han built on the site of a discarded park of Ch'in. It was vast and splendid with palaces and woodlands, having various functions and recreational facilities, rolling about 340 kilometers.

* *hsow*: a vertical bamboo flute.
* dragon: Though variously understood as a large reptile, a marine monster, a jackal and so on in Western culture, it has been esteemed as a fabulous serpent-like giant winged animal, a totem of the Chinese nation and a symbol of benevolence and sovereignty in Chinese culture.

其 四

玉树春归日，
金宫乐事多。
后庭朝未入，
轻辇夜相过。
笑出花间语，
娇来竹下歌。
莫教明月去，
留著醉嫦娥。

No. 4

The palace begins its night play
As trees see off the setting sun.
His Majesty's finished His day;
His sedan cart thru dusk does run,
The ladies laugh amid the flowers,
And sing softly in the bamboo.
To our hearts' content keep the moon,
And drink cupfuls to Luna woo.

* Luna: the moon, an important image in Chinese literature or culture as it can give rise to many associations such as solitude and nostalgia on the one hand, and purity, brightness and happy reunions on the other. What is "moon" in Chinese has at least two hundred names, like Jade Mound (yaot'ai), Fair Lady (ts'anchüan), Jade Hare (yüt'u), White Hare (pait'u), Silver Hare (yint'u), Ice Hare (pingt'u), Gold Hare (chint'u), Hare Gleam (t'uhui), Laurel Soul (Kuip'o) and so on.

其 五

绣户香风暖，
纱窗曙色新。
宫花争笑日，
池草暗生春。
绿树闻歌鸟，
青楼见舞人。
昭阳桃李月，
罗绮自相亲。

No. 5

The palace is warm with spring wind;
The window gauze takes in light new.
The garden flowers beguile the sun;
The pool grass adds to the spring hue.
The emerald trees hear birds sing;
The blue brothel sees singers dance.
Hall of Glare is greeting the dawn;
The belles go on with their romance.

* the blue brothel: of cultural significance in China, an elegant place for recreation, where singers and dancers entertain their client, usually selling their art instead of their body.

其 六

今日明光里，
还须结伴游。
春风开紫殿，
天乐下朱楼。
艳舞全知巧，
娇歌半欲羞。
更怜花月夜，
宫女笑藏钩。

No. 6

Today in this Bright Palace here
Together we need stroll to play.
The spring wind opens Purple Hall,
From Scarlet Tower alights a fay.
Dancers are dexterous and smart;
The moving songs seem to be shy.
More lovely is the moonlit night;
The belles sing *Hide Hooks on the Sly*.

* Bright Palace: name of a Han palace.
* Purple Hall: name of an imperial palace, alluding to the one built by Emperor Martial of Han
* Scarlet Tower: name of a deluxe building.
* *Hide Hooks on the Sly*: a song about a recreational activity in Emperor Deepsire's palace.

其 七

寒雪梅中尽，
春风柳上归。
宫莺娇欲醉，
檐燕语还飞。
迟日明歌席，
新花艳舞衣。
晚来移彩仗，
行乐泥光辉。

No. 7

Snow on wintersweets leaves no trace;
Spring wind comes back to willows spry.
The tender orioles seem so drunk;
The swallows on eaves chirp and fly.
The late sun glows to play and feast;
Their costumes greet the blossoms bright.
The afterglow paints the parade;
What a picture and what a sight!

* wintersweet: a cold-resistant plant having small yellow or red flowers, a symbol of elegance, solitude and pride in Chinese culture for its blossoming and fragrance in defiance of the coldest snowy winter while all other plants are still dry, bare and devoid of vitality.
* swallow: a passerine bird, with short broad, depressed bill, long pointed wings, and forked tail, noted for fleeting flight and migratory habits. In Chinese culture, swallows are welcome to live with families with their nest built on a beam.

其 八

水绿南薰殿,
花红北阙楼。
莺歌闻太液,
凤吹绕瀛洲。
素女鸣珠佩,
天人弄彩毬。
今朝风日好,
宜入未央游。

No. 8

Water greens South Lavender Hall;
Blossoms redden the north glazed tiles.
Orioles' chirps float to Nectar Pool;
A wind blows to the fairy isles.
The fairies' trinkets sway to clink;
The ladies play a colored ball.
What a nice day we have today!
Lets' play within the Non-end wall.

* South Lavender Hall: in Rise-Plaud Palace according to *Long Peace Records*.
* Nectar Pool: a pool in Great Bright Palace.
* Non-end: referring to Non-end Palace, a palace of the Han House, a metaphor for the imperial palace in this poem. Non-end Palace was built on the basis of Chapter Height, a Ch'in palace, in 200 B.C., monitored by Premier Ho Hsiao (257 B.C.- 193 B.C.), located on Dragonhead Plateau, the highest vantage of Long Peace. It was the political center of the Han Empire for 200 years and was made a part of the Forbidden Park in the Sui and T'ang dynasties. Non-end, six times as large as today's Forbidden City or Imperial Palace in Peking, existed for 1,041 years, the longest-lived palace in Chinese history.

清平调词三首
Pure Peace Tune, Three Poems

其 一

云想衣裳花想容，
春风扶槛露华浓。
若非群玉山头见，
会向瑶台月下逢。

No. 1

Her dress like plumage and her face a rose,
Breeze pets the rails and the belle in repose.
If not a fairy queen from Heav'n on high,
She's Goddess of Moon that makes rosebuds shy.

* Three Poems: Pai Li's poems composed impromptu at a royal party held by Emperor Deepsire with Lady Yang in the Pavilion of Aloes on a spring day. The tree-peonies newly imported from India were in full bloom as if in rivalry of beauty with the emperor's voluptuous mistress. There were the musicians of the Pear Garden and the wine of grapes from Coolton. Pai Li was summoned, because his art could capture for eternity the glory of the vanishing hours.
* the belle: referring to Jade Ring (A.D. 719 - A.D. 756), Deepsire the Emperor's Imperial Consort, a talented musician, one of the four beauties in Chinese history, the loveliest of the three thousand palace ladies of T'ang, ever accompanying the emperor's palanquin, singing and dancing to him.
* Goddess of Moon: Lord Alarm (Ti K'u)'s imperial concubine. Lord Alarm (2480 B.C.-2345 B.C.) was one of five mythical emperors in prehistorical China.

其 二

一枝红艳露凝香，
云雨巫山枉断肠。
借问汉宫谁得似？
可怜飞燕倚新妆。

No. 2

A rosebud red glistens with fragrant dew;
Such nymphs, on earth or Heav'n, are really few.
The beauty the duke craved couldn't compare;
Lady Chao, to shine, new clothes had to wear.

* nymph: alluding to the Goddess of Mt. Witch, who told King Hsiang of Ch'u that she was named Cloud in the morning and Rain in the evening in his dream, where they had the romance of sex.
* Flying Swallow: referring to Feiyan Chao (45 B.C.-1 B.C.). Starting as a dancer in the residence of Princess Yang'o, she attracted Emperor Complete of Han's attention, hence she was made an imperial concubine of the highest rank and then crowned as empress. She was famous for her frail beauty. It is said that she was of so slight a build that she could dance on the palm of the hand.

其 三

名花倾国两相欢，
长得君王带笑看。
解释春风无限恨，
沉香亭北倚阑干。

No. 3

The rose and reigning belle smile each to each;
His Majesty's eyes make a happy reach.
Thus dissolves the melancholy of breeze.
Balm flirting, they lean on the rail at ease.

* rose: any of a genus of shrubs of the rose family, characteristically with prickly stems, alternate compound leaves, and five-parted, usually fragrant flowers or red, pink, white, yellow, etc., having many stamens. It is often used as a metaphor for beauty or love.
* reigning belle: referring to Lady Yang, Emperor Deepsire's Imperial Consort called Jade Ring, a beautiful and talented woman who had all favor and grace from the emperor.
* His Majesty: referring to Emperor Deepsire (Hsuan Tsung) (A.D. 685 – A.D. 762), the ninth emperor of the T'ang dynasty. When a prince, he was regarded as wise and valiant, a sportsman accomplished in all knightly exercises and a master of all elegant arts. He established Pear Garden, an operatic school, where actors and actresses were trained, and the prototype of the modern Chinese drama was developed.

鼓吹入朝曲

金陵控海浦，
渌水带吴京。
铙歌列骑吹，
飒沓引公卿。
槌钟速严妆，
伐鼓启重城。
天子凭玉几，
剑履若云行。
日出照万户，
簪裾烂明星。
朝罢沐浴闲，
遨游阆风亭。
济济双阙下，
欢娱乐恩荣。

Attending Levee in Music

The seashore looks up to Gold Hill;
The capital loves her green rill.
On steeds is played a cymbal song;
Courtiers and grandees come along.
Tolls urge them to straight up their gown;
Drums hasten gatemen of the town.
By the jade desk sits the Most High;
All ministers like clouds come nigh.
The sun to all households does shine;

Their arrays gleam, brilliantly fine.
Levee o'er, they bathe there to rest,
Or stroll the court by wind caressed.
The beauties queue up in a line,
While basking in His grace divine.

* Gold Hill: referring to Nanking, one of the most well-known ancient cities in China, a strategic fort as a gateway to the sea, which has been the capital of Wu, Chin, and many other states or kingdoms, such as the six empires called Six Dynasties and has flourished immensely with increasing trade and travel.

秦女休行

西门秦氏女，
秀色如琼花。
手挥白杨刀，
清昼杀仇家。
罗袖洒赤血，
英声凌紫霞。
直上西山去，
关吏相邀遮。
婿为燕国王，
身被诏狱加。
犯刑若履虎，
不畏落爪牙。
素颈未及断，
摧眉卧泥沙。
金鸡忽放赦，
大辟得宽赊。
何惭聂政姐，
万古共惊嗟。

The Ch'in Belle Is Pardoned

A belle of the Ch'ins by West Gate
Outshines a rosebud or bright jade.
She waves up her White Poplar sword,
Hence in the morn her feud is slayed.
Her silken sleeves are stained with blood;

Her valor praised, good fame she's got.
She goes straightly to the West Hills,
And by the pass guards she is caught.
Her husband is the king of Yan,
But she's been by an order jailed.
Criminal punishment is harsh,
She's not afraid of being nailed.
Before she is cut by the neck
And buried low under the sand,
The golden rooster news arrives:
She has gotten a pardon grand.
Before Sis Nieh she's not abased;
Both of them are by the world praised.

* White Poplar sword: a kind of short broadsword.
* Sis Nieh: referring to Cheng Nieh's sister. Cheng Nieh was an assassin from Ch'i in the Warring States period. He, disfigured, committed suicide in a case implicating his sister after he completed the assassination. The Hans hung his body downtown to find out who he was. Sis Nieh heard of this and came to identify her brother without fear, and later took her own life besides Cheng.
* golden rooster news: rescript of amnesty. According to *The Sui Book*, prisoners were gathered at a golden rooster and drums placed at the right of the town gate and were released after drums were beaten a thousand times. And according to *The New T'ang Book*, a gold grooster was four feet tall, its head decorated with gold.

秦女卷衣

天子居未央，
妾侍卷衣裳。
顾无紫宫宠，
敢拂黄金床。
水至亦不去，
熊来尚可当。
微身奉日月，
飘若萤之光。
愿君采葑菲，
无以下体妨。

The Ch'in Belle Prepares His Array

The Lord bides in Non-end Palace,
His ladies His array prepare.
Without the favor of the Lord;
Who dare touch His gold bed, who dare?
Even if flood comes, one can't go;
If a bear attacks, she should fight.
All humbly serve the sun and moon
Like fireflies flickering their light.
When you gather cordata to eat,
Don't get roots but reject leaves sweet.

* Non-end: referring to Non-end Palace, a palace of the Han House, built on the basis of Chapter Height, a Ch'in palace, in 200 B.C., monitored by Premier Ho Hsiao (257

B.C.- 193 B.C.), located on Dragonhead Plateau, the highest vantage of Long Peace. It was the political center of the Han Empire for 200 years and was made a part of the Forbidden Park in the Sui and T'ang dynasties. Non-end, six times as large as today's Forbidden City or Imperial Palace in Peking, existed for 1,041 years, the longest-lived palace in Chinese history.

* Even if flood comes, one can't go: an allusion to King Glare of Chu's consort. When a flood came, the lady refused to leave with the official without the king's tally.
* If a bear attacks, she should fight: When Emperor Yüan of Han and his concubines enjoyed a beast fight, a bear burst out and frightened the ladies away. Only Lady Feng stood in front of the emperor and fought against the bear.
* firefly: any of a family (*Lampyridae*) of winged beetles, active at night, whose abdomens usually glow with a luminescent light.
* cordata: a kind of edible plant like turnip.

东 武 吟

好古笑流俗,
素闻贤达风。
方希佐明主,
长揖辞成功。
白日在高天,
回光烛微躬。
恭承凤凰诏,
欻起云萝中。
清切紫霄迥,
优游丹禁通。
君王赐颜色,
声价凌烟虹。
乘舆拥翠盖,
扈从金城东。
宝马丽绝景,
锦衣入新丰。
依岩望松雪,
对酒鸣丝桐。
因学扬子云,
献赋甘泉宫。
天书美片善,
清芬播无穷。
归来入咸阳,
谈笑皆王公。
一朝去金马,
飘落成飞蓬。
宾客日疏散,

玉樽亦已空。
才力犹可倚，
不惭世上雄。
闲作东武吟，
曲尽情未终。
书此谢知己，
吾寻黄绮翁。

Ode to Eastmight

The past I like, this world I flout;
Sages and saints I do admire.
I wish to serve a saintly lord
And on success I would retire.
The sun is glaring high above,
A-shedding warming light on me.
Blessed with an imperial edict,
I rise from grass, a clerk to be.
Then an important post I hold,
So free here with no check or stop.
His Majesty is kind to me;
My fame soars high to clouds atop.
His canopied cart I escort,
To and out of the bathing town.
I ride to this picturesque place,
And enter Newrich in silk gown.
I gaze at a pine by a rock,
And to the tune of lute toast wine.
I would learn from Man Yang in Han,
Who to Sweet Spring offered verse fine.

By His Majesty I am praised,
And my good fame travels afar.
I have come back now to Allshine;
Laughing, talking, grandees there are.
Once I go off from Gold Horse Gate,
I'll drift like thistledown, blown up.
Few friends or guests will come to me;
And I will hold my empty cup.
My aptitude I could count on;
With all talents I can compare.
Now idle, *East Martial* I croon;
My feeling stays though ends the air.
With this verse I thank all friends mine;
I'll wend to hills, cypress and pine.

* edict: a public ordinance emanating from a sovereign and having the force of law.
* Newrich: a county, located in the northeast of Lintung, well known for its good wine. The county was built by Pang Liu in imitation of his hometown Rich County, in today's Lintung County, Sha'anhsi Province.
* Man Yang (53 B.C.- A.D. 18): Hsiung Yang if transliterated, a great scholar, rhymed prose writer and official in the Han dynasty. His *The Great One* is a masterpiece, a literary genre between verse and prose, which can be termed as euph (a coinage based on euphuism and euphemism); it has had a deep influence on works of later generations. According to *History of the Han Dynasty*, when other officials flattered those in power, only Man Yang kept to himself to write his philosophical work, *The Great One*.
* Sweet Spring: an imperial resort in the Han dynasty, which had witnessed a great number of political activities.
* Allshine: the capital of the Empire of Ch'in. It was built in 350 B.C. and Ch'in moved its capital here the next year from Oakshine (Liyang).
* Gold Horse Gate: a gateway to Han's palace, where edicts were waited for.
* *East Martial*: a conservatoire tune.
* cypress and pine: two similar evergreen trees, often mentioned together, a symbol of rectitude, nobility and longevity in Chinese culture.

邯郸才人嫁为厮养卒妇

妾本丛台女，
扬蛾入丹阙。
自倚颜如花，
宁知有凋歇。
一辞玉阶下，
去若朝云没。
每忆邯郸城，
深宫梦秋月。
君王不可见，
惆怅至明发。

A Beauty from Hantan Married to a Servant

I'm a woman from Cluster Mound,
Having come to the court in glee.
I've been proud of my blooming face,
Who knows withered a bloom can be?
Once one goes down the high jade steps,
She'll be gone like dawning clouds soon.
I oft recall my life in Hantan,
A harem dream in the fall moon.
His Majesty I can't please now;
I sigh till daybreak, a sad brow.

* Hantan: one of the earliest cities in China, with a history of 3,100 years. As the capital of the State of Chao, it prospered for 180 years until subjugated in 228 B.C. and

annexed in 221 B.C. by Ch'in.
* Cluster Mound: referring to the royal palace of Chao in the Warring States period.
* jade steps: the steps before, and leading to, a palace hall or a harem, usually built with marble, jade being a metaphor for good quality, often used as a metonymy for the court.
* the moon: the celestial body that revolves around the earth from west to east as a satellite, which appears at night and gives off shining silvery light, an image of purity and solitude in Chinese culture.

出自蓟北门行

房阵横北荒,
胡星耀精芒。
羽书速惊电,
烽火昼连光。
虎竹救边急,
戎车森已行。
明主不安席,
按剑心飞扬。
推毂出猛将,
连旗登战场。
兵威冲绝幕,
杀气凌穹苍。
列卒赤山下,
开营紫塞旁。
孟冬风沙紧,
旌旗飒凋伤。
画角悲海月,
征衣卷天霜。
挥刃斩楼兰,
弯弓射贤王。
单于一平荡,
种落自奔亡。
收功报天子,
行歌归咸阳。

Out of the North Gate of Chi

The Huns form lines on the north wild;
The stars there sparkle bloody rays.
Reports come on like lightening;
Beacon fires remain nights and days.
The tallies are matched for the front;
The chariots begin to rumble.
His Majesty can't be assured;
Hand on sword, His heart does grumble.
Generals are boosted with good gifts;
Flags to the battlefield flow high.
The soldiers' power presses the sand;
Their morale soars over the sky.
Soldiers down the Red Hills line up;
Camps by the Purple Fortress stand.
First month of winter, wind blows hard;
Banners and flags are marred by sand.
Honks sound sad to the moon at sea;
Uniforms are frosted with snow.
King of Lowland's cut with a sword;
The chieftains are shot with a bow.
The enemies run off pell-mell
As soon as the chief is crushed down.
When victory's reported to Lord,
The troops sing back to Allshine Town.

* Hun: one of barbaric nomadic Asian peoples who frequently invaded China, a general term referring to all northern or western invaders and aliens.

* beacon fire: bonfire from a prominent building set on a wall or hill or a similar position, as a guide or warning to garrison generals or others.
* tallies: In ancient China, a military tally was used as a token issued to generals for troop movement. It was usually cut into two halves with one half kept by the sovereign and the other by local generals, and generals could send troops only if the two halves were matched.
* the Red Hills: thousands of kilometers southwest of East Liao, the area east of the Liao River, today's Liaoning Province.
* Purple Fortress: an alternative name for the Great Wall for its brick clay was purple.
* the moon: the satellite of the earth, a representation of feminity in contrast with the sun, a presentation of masculinity. In a universe animated by the interaction of Shade (female) and Shine (male) energies, the moon is literally Shade visible.
* Lowland: Kroraina, a small city-state in the western regions, specifically in the west of Lop Nor on the Silk Road, which was founded in 176 B.C. and mysteriously disappeared in A.D. 630.
* Allshine Town: the ancient capital of the State of Ch'in and later the Ch'in Empire, that is, present-day Hsienyang, Sha'anhsi Province.

洛 阳 陌

白玉谁家郎，
回车渡天津。
看花东陌上，
惊动洛阳人。

On the Thoroughfare in Loshine

Who is the fair skinned youngster there?
Thru Kingford Bridge he's driving down.
Viewing blooms on East Thoroughfare,
He startles the whole Loshine Town.

* Loshine: Loyang if transliterated, one of the four ancient capitals in China, along with Long Peace (Hsi'an), Gold Hill (Nanking) and Peking, and it was the second largest city and the eastern capital of the T'ang dynasty, with a population of 800,000. It was first built from 1735 B.C. to 1540 B.C. in the Hsia dynasty as its political center, and in 1046 B.C. Prince of Chough built two cities here in order to control Chough's east territory. In 770 B.C. King Peace of Chough moved to this place when Warmer (Haoching), Chough's capital, was captured by Hounds (Ch'üanjung), hence the Eastern Chough dynasty. Since its founding, Loshine has been a capital for thirteen dynasties.
* Kingford Bridge: a bridge of great importance in Loshine, which connected two prosperous blocks of the ancient city.

北 上 行

北上何所苦？
北上缘太行。
磴道盘且峻，
巉岩凌穹苍。
马足蹶侧石，
车轮摧高冈。
沙尘接幽州，
烽火连朔方。
杀气毒剑戟，
严风裂衣裳。
奔鲸夹黄河，
凿齿屯洛阳。
前行无归日，
返顾思旧乡。
惨戚冰雪里，
悲号绝中肠。
尺布不掩体，
皮肤剧枯桑。
汲水涧谷阻，
采薪陇坂长。
猛虎又掉尾，
磨牙皓秋霜。
草木不可餐，
饥饮零露浆。
叹此北上苦，
停骖为之伤。
何日王道平，

开颜睹天光?

Going Up North

Going up north is hard, so hard,
Going up, by Mt. Great Go high.
The steps winding up and so steep,
The crags rising to the blue sky.
Horse shoes kick off pebbles aside;
Wheels roll on and crash the high mound.
Sand storms whirl in the border state;
Beacon fires stretch away, northbound.
Swords and halberds shine, bloody cold;
A harsh wind blows and tears the gown.
The Yellow River sees whales swarm,
Zigzagging along Loshine Town.
Just going, no chance to return,
Head turned, how we burn to go back!
Struggling so hard with ice and snow,
We cannot bear the pain, alack.
Clothing not enough to keep warm,
Mulberry twigs my coarse skin prong.
I'd fetch water, but the dale's deep;
I'd get firewood, but the slope's long.
Ferocious tigers may catch up,
Showing their sharp teeth with no blink.
Bushes and grass we cannot eat;
Liquids and dew we try to drink.
Going up north is a hard trip,
I stop my chariot for a sigh.

> When can we have a peaceful world,
> Basking in the light from the sky?

* Mt. Great Go: Mt. T'aihang if transliterated, meandering on the border of Shanhsi, Honan and Sha'anhsi, an important mountain range in East China and a geographic dividing line.
* beacon fire: bonfire from a beacon tower, a prominent building set on a wall or hill or a similar position, as a guide or warning to garrison generals or others.
* Loshine Town: Loshine, the second largest city and the east capital of T'ang, at which time it had about 800,000 inhabitants.
* mulberry: the edible, berry-like fruit of a tree (genus *Morus*) whose leaves are valued for silkworm culture, and the tree itself, first cultivated in the drainage area of the Yellow River in China about five thousand years ago.
* the Yellow River: the second longest river in China, the cradle of Chinese civilization. As legend goes, the river derived from a yellow dragon that, couchant on Midland Plain, ate yellow soil, flooded crops, devoured people and stock, and was finally tamed by Great Worm, the First King of Hsia (cir. 21 B.C.- 16 B.C.).
* tiger: a large carnivorous feline mammal of Asia, with vertical black wavy stripes on a tawny body and black bars or rings on the limbs and tail, praised as king of all animals.

短 歌 行

白日何短短，
百年苦易满。
苍穹浩茫茫，
万劫太极长。
麻姑垂两鬓，
一半已成霜。
天公见玉女，
大笑亿千场。
吾欲揽六龙，
回车挂扶桑。
北斗酌美酒，
劝龙各一觞。
富贵非所愿，
与人驻颜光。

A Short Song

How short, how short and fast a day!
A hundred years' pains go away.
The dome has no borders around;
An aeon stretches on without bound.
Maid Flax does her sideburns portray,
Half of it white, half of it gray.
Lord Heaven for fun, with Jade Maid,
Thru countless laughs, pot game has played.
I would, with Six Dragons beside,

Turn east and then to Mulberry ride.
The Dipper used for mellow wine,
Each dragon drinks a cup to dine.
Renown is not what I wish for;
May people keep their prime in store.

* aeon: an endlessly long period of time, which may consist of many kalpas. In Vedic scripture, a kalpa is a worldcycle lasting 4,320,000 years.
* Maid Flax: an immortal, a symbol of longevity.
* Lord Heaven: the supreme lord in Heaven, comparable to God in western culture.
* Jade Maid: a fairy that waits upon Lord Heaven.
* Six Dragons: referring to the sun. In Chinese legend, a goddess named She-her rides a cart pulled by six dragons across the sky every day to bring light to the world.
* Mulberry: a mythical tree growing in East Sea and the sun rises from where it stands.
* the Dipper: a constellation composed of seven bright stars, which looks like a spoon in the sky.
* wine: one of the most important beverages in Chinese culture, of which brown wine was brewed more than three thousand years ago and white wine (spirit) became popular in the Sung dynasty. Wine has an important position in Chinese life, such as literary creation, cultural activities, health care, cookery and so on.

空 城 雀

嗷嗷空城雀,
身计何戚促。
本与鹪鹩群,
不随凤皇族。
提携四黄口,
饮乳未尝足。
食君糠秕馀,
常恐乌鸢逐。
耻涉太行险,
羞营覆车粟。
天命有定端,
守分绝所欲。

Sparrows o'er the Town

Sparrows chirp o'er the empty town;
With nothing to live on, they frown.
With wrens they would flock together,
Different from the phoenix feather.
Four fledglings they try best to brood,
So little means, so little food.
Chaff they eat, residue they bite;
They're oft worried with a black kite.
To steep peaks they're afraid to dart;
They shrink at grains dropped from a cart.
Heavens above o'er all preside;

In solitude they would abide.

* sparrow: a small, plain-colored passerine bird related to the finches, grosbeaks and buntings, a very common bird in China, a symbol of insignificance.
* wren: any of numerous small passerine birds, having short rounded wings and a short tail.
* black kite: any of the birds of prey of the hawk family.
* Heavens o'er all preside: Heavens, standing for omnipotence of the personalized Word or God, decides everything in the universe and beyond.

菩萨蛮

平林漠漠烟如织,
寒山一带伤心碧。
暝色入高楼,
有人楼上愁。
玉阶空伫立,
宿鸟归飞急。
何处是归程?
长亭连短亭。

Bodhisattva Bun

The even wood rolls in mist like cloth spread;
The chilly hill's aggrieved like a green thread.
Dusk creeps into the tower so high;
Someone inside the tower does sigh.
On the jade steps she waits in vain;
The birds fly back to their nest again.
Where is my way back home to run?
The high kiosk links with a short one.

× jade steps: the steps before, and leading to, a palace hall or a harem, usually built with marble, jade being a metaphor for good quality, often used as a metonymy for the court. A verse titled *Pear Blossoms in the Left Office* by another T'ang poet mentions the steps jade white, as reads: "The chill of theirs bullies the frost; / Their fragrance soaks into the night. / As spring wind blows, tossing and tossed, / They fly over the steps jade white."

忆 秦 娥

箫声咽,
秦娥梦断秦楼月。
秦楼月,
年年柳色,
灞陵伤别。
乐游原上清秋节,
咸阳古道音尘绝。
音尘绝,
西风残照,
汉家陵阙。

Missing Fair Ch'in

A sad flute tune,
Fair Ch'in bemoans the tower moon clear,
The tower moon clear.
Willows turn green each year
At Paridge, they part in tear.
On the Glee Play Plain, the autumn is drear;
From Allshine Broadway all souls disappear,
Souls disappear.
West wind through the dusk glow
Blows to the Han tombs drear.

* flute: a tubular wind instrument of small diameter with holes along the side.
* Fair Ch'in: a singing girl; a daughter of Lord Solemn of Ch'in.

* willow: any of a large genus of shrubs and trees related to the poplars, widely distributed in China and most of the world, having glossy green leaves resembling a girl's eye-brow, and generally having smooth branches, and often long, slender, pliant, and sometimes pendent branchlets, which seem to be waving good-bye, or weeping amorously, or drooping for nostalgia. The best image is in *Vetch We Pick*, a verse in *The Book of Songs*, which is like this: When we left long ago, / The willows waved adieu. / Now back to our home town, / We meet snow falling down.
* Paridge: the ancient name of Yüehshine, where Emperor Civil of Han was buried.
* Glee Play Plain: the highest mound in Long Peace in the T'ang dynasty.
* Allshine Broadway: about 100 kilometers northwest of Long Peace, a main road for military and business purposes in the Han and T'ang dynasties.

乐府三十八首
Conservatoire, 38 Poems

发 白 马

将军发白马,
旌节渡黄河。
箫鼓聒川岳,
沧溟涌涛波。
武安有震瓦,
易水无寒歌。
铁骑若雪山,
饮流涸滹沱。
扬兵猎月窟,
转战略朝那。
倚剑登燕然,
边烽列嵯峨。
萧条万里外,
耕作五原多。
一扫清大漠,
包虎戢金戈。

Starting from Whitehorse Ford

The general starts from Whitehorse Ford;
His flags the Yellow River cross.
Conks and drums shake hills and rills;
Like the sea its breakers does toss.
The sound will break Warpeace's tiles;
There's no cold song o'er the Change now.
The steeds move like mountains of snow;

They'll drink the river dry, they vow.
The troops hunt at Moon Den in west,
And then they capture Ch'uno Town.
With their swords they climb Mt. Yanjan,
Whereon beacons line up and down.
The Great Wall's bleak for miles and miles;
The folks are tilling the plain wide.
The soldiers sweep the wild with force,
Their gold spears wrapped in tiger hide.

* Whitehorse Ford: a ferry on the southern bank of the Yellow River, 5 kilometers from today's Hua County, Honan Province.
* the Yellow River: the second longest river in China, a birthplace of Chinese civilization. As legend goes, the river derived from a yellow dragon that, couchant on Midland Plain, ate yellow soil, flooded crops, devoured people and stock, and was finally tamed by Great Worm, the First King of Hsia (cir. 21 B.C.- 16 B.C.).
* Warpeace tiles: The State of Ch'in sent forces to dominate the State of Han, and stationed the troops at the west of Warpeace. Their forces were so strong that as they drummed, the tiles in Warpeace even broke due to the sound.
* cold song o'er the Change: When K'e Ching the assassin from Yan started off to kill King of Ch'in, the Prince of Yan and K'e Ching's friend Chienli Kao sang a song to bid him farewell at the cold River Change: "The Change River's cold, while wind blows to sough; / The brave man won't return o, as he's leaving now".
* steed: a horse; especially a spirited war horse. The use of horses in war can be traced back to the Shang dynasty (1600 B.C.- 1046 B.C.), when a department of horse management was established. A verse from *The Book of Songs* tells of Lord Civil of Watch's industriousness: "In state affairs he leads; / He has three thousand steeds."
* Moon Den: referring to the extreme western land.
* And then they capture Ch'uno Town: In 166 B.C., Hun's troops 140 thousand strong conquered Ch'uno Town.
* Mt. Yanjan: a mountain located in present-day Mongolia. It is usually used to imply an enemy with military threat.
* the Great Wall: usually called Ten Thousand Li Great Wall, a giant project undertaken in different periods of Chinese history, generally from Ch'in (221 B.C.- 207 B.C.) to Ming (A.D. 1368 - A.D. 1644), to defend China from northern nomadic invasions.

陌 上 桑

美女渭桥东，
春还事蚕作。
五马如飞龙，
青丝结金络。
不知谁家子，
调笑来相谑。
妾本秦罗敷，
玉颜艳名都。
绿条映素手，
采桑向城隅。
使君且不顾，
况复论秋胡。
寒螀爱碧草，
鸣凤栖青梧。
托心自有处，
但怪傍人愚。
徒令白日暮，
高驾空踟蹰。

The Mulberry Gatherer

The beauty east of the Wei bridge
Picks mulberry leaves, a job in spring.
A five-horsed cart runs and stops here,
Each harness tied with a green string.
Who is this fop, from where is he

Who has come here to laugh and jest?
This girl is Lofu Ch'in by name;
In this town she's a dream, the best.
Green leaves shine to her tender hand,
As she picks mulberries by the wall.
The high official can't move her,
Nor can Cutewho succeed at all.
Phoenixes love parasol trees;
Chilly cicadas like green grass.
She has someone deep in her heart,
But they cannot see it, alas.
They've waited for her all in vain,
Pacing forward and back again.

* mulberry: the edible, berry-like fruit of a tree (genus *Morus*) whose leaves are valued for silkworm culture, and the tree itself, first cultivated in the drainage area of the Yellow River in China about five thousand years ago.
* the Wei: the Wei River: the largest branch of the Yellow River, originating from today's Mt. Birdmouse in Kansu Province, flowing through Precious Rooster, Allshine, Long Peace, and meeting the Yellow River at T'ung Pass.
* A five-horsed cart: a cart usually designated for a prefecture chief.
* Luofu Ch'in: a belle in the Han dynasty. She behaved gracefully even if a prefecture chief flirted with her.
* Cutewho: a man from Lu in the Spring and Autumn period. He left for Ch'en to assume his duty the fifth day after his wedding. Five years later, he returned. Seeing a beauty picking mulberry leaves on the roadside, he flirted with her by giving her gold but she refused. When the flirter arrived home, he found that his wife was exactly the beauty on the roadside. His wife, reprimanding him for having flirted with a woman, jumped into a river out of rage.
* parasol tree: Chinese parasol tree (*Firmiana simplex*), tree of the hibiscus family native to Asia, growing as tall as 12 metres, having deciduous leaves and small greenish white flowers that are borne in clusters.
* cicada: a homopterous insect that sings its song of summer and shrills in autumn, a

symbol of death and resurrection in Chinese culture because of its metamorphosis and recycle. Therefore, in ancient China, a jade cicada figure was put in the mouth of a dead body with such an intention of eternal life.

枯鱼过河泣

白龙改常服,
偶被豫且制。
谁使尔为鱼,
徒劳诉天帝。
作书报鲸鲵,
勿恃风涛势。
涛落归泥沙,
翻遭蝼蚁噬。
万乘慎出入,
柏人以为诫。

The Wounded Fish Cries

The white dragon oft changing clothes
Once gets pierced by a fishing rod.
Why did you change into a fish?
All in vain, you complain to God.
I'll write a letter to the whale,
To tell it: don't splash waves and roar.
You may get stranded at the ebb;
Ants and mole crickets may you gnaw.
Your Majesty should take great care;
Of traps and snipes you'd be aware.

* dragon: a fabulous serpent-like giant winged animal, a symbol of benevolence and sovereignty in Chinese culture.

* The white dragon oft changing clothes: an allusion to the remonstrance of Tzuhsu Wu, the renowned minister of Wu, who told a story that the white dragon lost its eyes because it was disguised as a fish.
* ant: a small social hymenopterous insect (family Formicidae), an emmet. The communities of ants, well organized according to their duties, are made up of winged males, females winged till after pairing and wingless neuters or workers.
* mole cricket: a burrowing cricket with a soft, cylindrical body and broad, mole-like front legs, found in some sandy soils.

丁督护歌

云阳上征去,
两岸饶商贾。
吴牛喘月时,
拖船一何苦!
水浊不可饮,
壶浆半成土。
一唱都护歌,
心摧泪如雨。
万人系磐石,
无由达江浒。
君看石芒砀,
掩泪悲千古。

The Song of Captain

I boat up to Cloudshine, upstream;
The banks with businesses teem.
The buffalo breathes to the moon;
The boat tuggers do sadly croon.
The turbid water one can't drink;
The pot's full of mud, to the brink.
The Song of Captain they now sing,
And feel tears dripping like a string.
Ten thousand mining the boulder
Can't move it soon to the river.
Look at those for aragonite;

How wretched they are now in plight!

* Cloudshine: Cloudshine County, renamed Redshine in Deepsire's reign, that is, modern-day Redshine (Tanyang), Chiangsu Province.
* The buffalo breathes to the moon: The buffalo is a large ox often staying in water, now extensively domesticated, having horns that broaden at the base. The buffalo lives in the southern land, but it fears summer heat. When it sees the moon at night, so frightened, it may take it as the sun, so it often gasps for a breath to the moon.
* the moon: the planet of the earth, which appears at night and gives off shining silvery light, an image of purity and solitude in Chinese culture.
* *the Song of Captain*: an ancient song expressing the feeling of sadness and sorrow.

相　逢　行

朝骑五花马，
谒帝出银台。
秀色谁家子，
云车珠箔开。
金鞭遥指点，
玉勒近迟回。
夹毂相借问，
疑从天上来。
蹙入青绮门，
当歌共衔杯。
衔杯映歌扇，
似月云中见。
相见不得亲，
不如不相见。
相见情已深，
未语可知心。
胡为守空闺，
孤眠愁锦衾。
锦衾与罗帷，
缠绵会有时。
春风正澹荡，
暮雨来何迟。
愿因三青鸟，
更报长相思。
光景不待人，
须臾发成丝。
当年失行乐，

老去徒伤悲。
持此道密意，
毋令旷佳期。

Seeing Her

On the morn, a piebald I ride
And from Silver Mound Gate depart.
I would ask whose beauty she is,
Out of the window of the cart.
My gold whip I wave and go near;
My horse wonders and lingers by.
This beauty I make bold to ask:
Are you a fairy from the sky?
I invite her to the green door
And we sing a song o'er the cup.
With a fan she hides half her face,
As if drunk with clouds hanging up.
Having seen but not getting close,
I would better not have you seen.
Having met, we are now in love;
Not speaking, we know what we mean.
Why should she keep her boudoir void
And in her silk quilt lonely stay?
O silk quilt and brocade curtain,
You will have your romance some day.
But now spring is right on the tide,
And a rain falls late from above.
May Mother West's messenger bird
Report my yearning and my love.

O time and tide wait for no man;
Our hair will soon turn gray and dry.
If we don't make merry while young,
When old, in vain we'll sadly sigh.
My sweet word to her please convey:
Take care, do not miss our best day.

* Silver Mound Gate: a palace gate.
* Mother West: a sovereign goddess living on Mt. Queen in Chinese myths. Her appearance was originally described as human-bodied, tiger-toothed, leopard-tailed and hoopoe-haired. Mother West is regarded as a goddess in charge of women protection, marriage and procreation, and longevity.

千 里 思

李陵没胡沙，
苏武还汉家。
迢迢五原关，
朔雪乱边花。
一去隔绝国，
思归但长嗟。
鸿雁向西北，
因书报天涯。

Missing the One

Ridge Li was buried in Hun sand;
Wu Su came back to Han at last.
The Five Plain Pass is far away,
Where a flurry whirls with a blast.
I'm kept so far off from my land;
Yearning for home, I heave a sigh.
Wild geese fly northwest every year;
May they send my letter thereby.

* Ridge Li: Ling Li (134 B.C.- 74 B.C.), the grandson of the outstanding General Broad Li. Ridge Li surrendered to the Huns after defeat, and completely broke off with the Han court when Lord Martial killed his family, believing the rumor.
* Hun: one of barbaric nomadic Asian peoples who frequently invaded China, a general term referring to all northern or western invaders or aliens.
* Wu Su: Wu Su (140 B.C.- 60 B.C.), a minister of Han. On his diplomatic mission, Su was detained. The Huns tried to make him surrender with threats and promises, only to

fail. Then, he was sent to North Sea to be a shepherd. Through all kinds of hardship, Su finally came back to Han after 19 years' detention. During the 19 years, Wu Su had never surrendered.

* the Five Plain Pass: name of a pass in today's Inner Mongolia.
* wild goose: an undomesticated goose that is caring and responsible, taken as a symbol of benevolence, righteousness, good manner, wisdom, and faith in Chinese culture.

树 中 草

鸟衔野田草,
误入枯桑里。
客土植危根,
逢春犹不死。
草木虽无情,
因依尚可生。
如何同枝叶,
各自有枯荣。

Grass in the Woods

The bird that holds grass in its bill
By mistake falls to mulberries dry.
A plant rooted in foreign soil,
With the care of spring, will not die.
Plants and grass, tho not human,
Each leaning on each, can survive.
With the same kind of twigs and leaves,
Why do some fade while others thrive?

君 马 黄

君马黄,
我马白。
马色虽不同,
人心本无隔。
共作游冶盘,
双行洛阳陌。
长剑既照曜,
高冠何赩赫。
各有千金裘,
俱为五侯客。
猛虎落陷阱,
壮士时屈厄。
相知在急难,
独好亦何益。

Yellow, Steed Thine

Yellow, steed thine,
And white, steed mine.
Horses may have a different hue,
There's no bar between me and you.
Together we travel and play,
Abreast along Loshine's broad way.
Behold, your long sword, how it glares!
Look at my high crown, how it flares!
Each wears a fur coat worth so much;

All are nobles, high ranked as such.
Tigers may fall into a trap;
Heroes can't go without mishap.
If you don't help someone in need,
How can you be a friend indeed?

* steed: a horse; especially a spirited war horse. The use of horses in war can be traced back to the Shang dynasty (1600 B.C.- 1046 B.C.), when a department of horse management was established. A verse from *The Book of Songs* tells of Lord Civil of Watch's industriousness: "In state affairs he leads; / He has three thousand steeds."
* Loshine: Loyang if transliterated, one of the four ancient capitals in China, along with Long Peace (Hsi'an), Gold Hill (Nanking) and Peking, and it was the second largest city and the east capital of T'ang.
* tiger: a large carnivorous feline mammal of Asia, with vertical black wavy stripes on a tawny body and black bars or rings on the limbs and tail, praised as king of all animals.

拟　古

融融白玉辉，
映我青蛾眉。
宝镜似空水，
落花如风吹。
出门望帝子，
荡漾不可期。
安得黄鹤羽，
一报佳人知。

In Ancient Style

Glitter, glitter, the jade so white
Sheds on my brows a streak of light.
The mirror like water does shine;
The blossom to the wind does whine.
Outdoors, to Grand and Bloom I peer;
Both of them far away appear.
Where can I find a yellow crane
So that they can my news attain?

* Grand and Bloom: Fairgrand and Shebloom in full name, the daughters of Mound (chief of tribal alliance in early historical times) (2377 B.C.- 2259 B.C.) according to lengend. They were married to their father's successor Hibiscus (cir. 2277 B.C.- cir. 2178 B.C.) and were drowned in the River Hsiang during their tour to find their husband who were on expedition. Later generations called them Madams Hsiang because their spirits lingered on the south of Lake Cavehall and the banks of the River Hsiang.

* crane: one of a family of large, long-necked, long legged, heronlike birds allied to the rails, a symbol of integrity and longevity in Chinese culture, only second to the phoenix in cultural importance.

折 杨 柳

垂杨拂绿水,
摇艳东风年。
花明玉关雪,
叶暖金窗烟。
美人结长想,
对此心凄然。
攀条折春色,
远寄龙庭前。

Plucking a Willow Twig

The willow stirs the water green,
Swaying in the breeze its sallow.
The blooms light up snow of Jade Pass;
The belle leans against her window.
Seeing the leaves and mist, she thinks,
A little bit under the harrow.
She would pluck a twig of spring hue,
Wherewith to pass him her sorrow.

* willow: any of a large genus of shrubs and trees related to the poplars, having generally smooth branches, and often long, slender, pliant, and sometimes pendent branchlets, which seem to be bidding farewell or weeping amorously or drooping for nostalgia.
* Jade Pass: an important military fort and passage on the Silk Road, built in the Han dynasty. It was so named because of jade trade between Han and the western regions as far as Europe.

少 年 子

青云少年子，
挟弹章台左。
鞍马四边开，
突如流星过。
金丸落飞鸟，
夜入琼楼卧。
夷齐是何人，
独守西山饿。

A Youngster

A youngster with black-clouded hair
With pellets hunts by Letter Height.
His horse neighs to gallop ahead,
Shooting like a meteor so bright.
This nude shoots down a flying bird
And enters a tower for the night.
Who were Bowone and Straightthree there,
Getting starved in so wretched plight?

× Letter Height: a Ch'in palace and the name of a street in the capital of Han, i.e., Long Peace.
* Bowone and Straightthree: men with noble characters, who left King Martial of Chough as they failed to admonish him and refused to take crops reaped under the sovereignty of Chough. They lived on fungi on Mt. Firstshine and starved to death in the end.

紫骝马

紫骝行且嘶，
双翻碧玉蹄。
临流不肯渡，
似惜锦障泥。
白雪关山远，
黄云海戍迷。
挥鞭万里去，
安得念春闺。

The Brown Horse

The brown horse gallops with a neigh,
Turning its jade hoofs up and down.
But it won't go across the stream,
Lest its satin shield will there drown.
The White Snow Pass is there, far off;
The Cloud Post far off he can't see.
He would crack his whip to fly on,
Leaving her in her bower to be.

* brown horse: the name of a fine horse in ancient times, often mentioned in poems.
* jade hoof: beautiful hoof, jade used as a metaphor like gold in English because jade was something precious monopolized by royal families in ancient China.
* satin shield: an auxiliary of a saddle.
* the White Snow Pass: a troop station in the T'ang dynasty.
* the Cloud Post: a troop station in the T'ang dynasty.

少年行二首

The Young Man, Two Poems

其 一

击筑饮美酒,
剑歌易水湄。
经过燕太子,
结托并州儿。
少年负壮气,
奋烈自有时。
因击鲁句践,
争博勿相欺。

No. 1

Plucking the *quin*, spirit drinking;
Playing the sword, seaside singing.
Making friends like Prince Tan of Yan;
Going high with Pingchow's true man.
This young man would go a long way;
He will fly high with might some day.
When best rivals come for a game,
They should not each other disclaim.

---

* Plucking the *quin*, spirit drinking: When K'e Ching the assassin from Yan started off to kill King of Ch'in, the Prince of Yan and K'e Ching's friend Chienli Kao came to bid him farewell. At the River Change, Kao played the *quin*, and Ching sang a stirring song.
* *quin*: an ancient Chinese musical instrument with five strings like a quinton.

* Prince Tan of Yan: the crown prince of Yan. After the State of Ch'in wiped out the State of Han and Chao, he sent K'e Ching to assassinate King of Ch'in.
* Pingchow: one of the nine administrative regions in ancient China, located roughly in the State of Yan including present-day Peking, Tientsin, the northern part of Hopei and the western part of Liaoning.

其 二

五陵年少金市东，
银鞍白马度春风。
落花踏尽游何处，
笑入胡姬酒肆中。

No. 2

Five Hills sees lads east of Gold Market play;
Spring tints their silver saddled steeds tip-top.
Having seen all blossoms, where will they go?
They will laugh with Hun girls in the wine shop.

* Five Hills: originally referring to the place where five Han emperors were buried. This place so thrived that many powerful or high-ranking people dwelt here.
* Gold Market: an alternative name of West Market of Long Peace for there was gold exchange business.
* Hun girls: foreign girls from west or north of China, some of whom were of Caucasian extraction, often selling wine in wine shops in the T'ang dynasty, featured with a high nose, charming eyes and brimming with enthusiasm and ardor.

白 鼻 騧

银鞍白鼻騧，
绿地障泥锦。
细雨春风花落时，
挥鞭直就胡姬饮。

White-nosed Brown Horse

Silver saddle, white-nosed brown steed,
Embroidered mud shield called green mead.
When spring wind blows a rain and petals drop,
He'll crack his whip to toast Hun girls tip-top.

* mud shield: an auxilliary placed by a saddle.
* Hun girls: foreign girls from west or north of China, often selling wine and giving performances in wine shops in the T'ang dynasty, featured with a high nose, charming eyes and brimming with enthusiasm and ardor.

豫 章 行

胡风吹代马,
北拥鲁阳关。
吴兵照海雪,
西讨何时还。
半渡上辽津,
黄云惨无颜。
老母与子别,
呼天野草间。
白马绕旌旗,
悲鸣相追攀。
白杨秋月苦,
早落豫章山。
本为休明人,
斩虏素不闲。
岂惜战斗死,
为君扫凶顽。
精感石没羽,
岂云惮险艰。
楼船若鲸飞,
波荡落星湾。
此曲不可奏,
三军鬓成斑。

The Yüchang Hill

The northern wind blows to Tai steeds,

And up to Sun Pass of Lu speeds.
The Wu soldiers march against snow
To the west front to fight the foe.
The ford in Liao the troops wade thru;
The yellow clouds turn palely blue.
When sons leave their mothers, alas,
They cry to the sky from wild grass.
Around the flags white steeds jump high;
They chase each other and they cry.
The poplars sad, the moon looks chill;
It sinks beyond the Yüchang Hill.
In great peace I was born and grow,
So unused to fighting the foe.
In the front I will thrust my sword
And kill those diehards for the Lord.
Earnestness can move stone to tears;
How can we say pains may cause fears!
Like whales, the tower boats ahead fly;
In Star Fall Bay waves surge high.
This moody air I could not play;
The troops have grown old, their hair gray.

* Tai steeds: a breed of fine horses, largely of greys, from an old prefecture called Tai on the Tartar borderlands of North China.
* Sun Pass of Lu: 40 kilometers north of Hsiangch'eng County in today's Honan Province.
* The ford in Liao, a ford in Yüchang Shire.
* poplar: any of a genus (*Populus*) of dioecious trees and bushes of the willow family, widely distributed in the northern hemisphere.
* the moon: the celestial body that revolves around the earth from west to east as a satellite, which appears at night and gives off shining silvery light, an image of purity and solitude in Chinese culture.

* the Yüchang Hill: a hill in Yüchang Shire, that is, Hsiushui County, Chianghsi Province.
* whale: a cetaceous mammal of fish-like form, especially one of the larger pelagic species, as distinguished from dolphins and porpoises. Whales have the fore limbs developed as broad flattened paddles, hind limbs absent, and a thick layer of fat or blubber immediately beneath the skin. A whale is a symbol of great ambition, fortitude and uniqueness.
* Star Fall Bay: also known as Star Fall Lake, northwest of P'oshine Lake in today's Chianghsi Province.

沐 浴 子

沐芳莫弹冠，
浴兰莫振衣。
处世忌太洁，
至人贵藏晖。
沧浪有钓叟，
吾与尔同归。

When Taking a Bath

Washing your hair, dust not your hat;
Taking your bath, don't your clothes pat.
In life, one should not be so clean;
The noblest man will hide his sheen.
O fisherman, how waves you ply!
Now let's go back there, you and I.

---

* The poem summarizes the different thoughts between Yüan Ch'ü, the patriotic minister of Ch'u, and a fisherman. The fisherman saw Yüan Ch'ü look withered and tortured for the twisted world, and he tried to persuade him to let it be. Yüan Ch'ü stuck to himself by telling the fisherman: "He who washes his hair must clean his hat; he who takes bath must pat his clothes. Only in this way can he stay clean." The fisherman replied, singing this song: "The water's limpid, wherewith I wash my lash; the water's turbid, wherewith I wash my feet." And he left Yüan Ch'ü behind.

高 句 骊

金花折风帽，
白马小迟回。
翩翩舞广袖，
似鸟海东来。

Koreans

Their caps adorned with blossoms gold,
Their white steeds trot and turn with glee.
The women wave their long long sleeves,
As if birds come back from East Sea.

* East Sea: what is known as East China Sea today, with an area of 770 thousand square kilometers.
* steed: a horse; especially a spirited war horse. The use of horses in war can be traced back to the Shang dynasty (1600 B.C.- 1046 B.C.), when a department of horse management was established. A verse from *The Book of Songs* tells of Lord Civil of Watch's industriousness: "In state affairs he leads; / He has three thousand steeds."

静 夜 思

床前看月光，
疑是地上霜。
举头望山月，
低头思故乡。

Night Thought

The moon sheds light before the bed,
Which seems to be frost on the ground.
To the bright moon, I raise my head,
And lower it to muse, for home bound.

* the moon: the satellite of the earth, an important image in Chinese literature or culture as it can evoke many associations such as solitude and nostalgia on the one hand, and purity, brightness and happy reunions on the other. In traditional times, there used to be a "moon-viewing party," at which people sat quietly on a moonlit night, particularly under a full moon, and thought of a loved one or loved ones far away, inside the vast reaches of China proper and even overseas, who might themselves be sitting sharing the same moon at the same time, in the same reverent silence.
* the bed: probably a flower bed in a yard, because looking at the moon in a room seems to be improbable.

渌 水 曲

渌水明秋月，
南湖采白蘋。
荷花娇欲语，
愁杀荡舟人。

Blue Water

The blue water gleams the moon bright;
South Lake sees girls pick duckweed white.
The lotuses would something say,
But the boatman feels sad, oh, nay.

* lotus: one of the various plants of the waterlily family, characterized by their large floating round leaves and showy flowers, especially the white or pink Asian lotus, used as a religious symbol in Hinduism and Buddhism. In Chinese culture, it is a symbol of purity and elegance, unsoiled though out of soil, so clean with all leaves green, is a common image in Chinese literature, as two lines of a lyric by Hsiu Ouyang (A.D. 1007 - A.D. 1072) read: "A thunder brings rain to the wood and pool, / The rain hushes the lotus, drips cool."
* duckweed white: Duckweed flowers in the fifth moon and the flowers are white, hence the name.

凤 凰 曲

嬴女吹玉箫，
吟弄天上春。
青鸾不独去，
更有携手人。
影灭彩云断，
遗声落西秦。

A Phoenix Song

Lord of Ch'in's girl plays the flute fair,
Blowing a spring lay, a spring air.
Alone the phoenix will not fly,
As if someone dear would come by.
The clouds engulf all their shadows
And in West Ch'in ring their echos.

* Lord of Ch'in's girl: referring to the daughter of Lord Solemn of Ch'in, who was good at playing the flute. Once in her dream she came across a young man riding a phoenix to play music with her. So Lord Solemn found the young man and married his daughter to him.
* flute: a tubular wind instrument of small diameter with holes along the side.
* Phoenix: In Chinese myths, phoenixes, auspicious birds, unlike ordinary ones, only perch on parasol trees, and only eat bamboo shoots and pearly stone.

凤 台 曲

尝闻秦帝女，
传得凤凰声。
是日逢仙子，
当时别有情。
人吹彩箫去，
天借绿云迎。
曲在身不返，
空馀弄玉名。

A Tune of Phoenix Mound

As I hear, Lord of Ch'in's girl played
A phoenix's love so well conveyed.
She met with a fairy that day,
What an encounter, what a play.
She blew the colored flute and soared,
Welcomed by clouds from Heaven's Lord.
The tune's here but she ne'er back came;
We only know Flute Maid, her name.

* Tune of Phoenix Mound: a Han conservatoire tune.
* Lord of Ch'in's girl: a daughter of Lord Solemn of Ch'in, who was good at playing the flute.
* phoenix: In Chinese myths, phoenixes, auspicious birds, unlike ordinary ones, only perch on parasol trees, and only eat bamboo shoots and pearly stone.
* Heaven's Lord: the ultimate being, God whose abode is Heaven, the space surrounding or seeming to overarch the earth, in which the sun, the moon, and stars appear.
* Flute Maid: Lord Solemn of Ch'in's daughter, who went to Heaven, playing the flute.

从 军 行

从军玉门道，
逐虏金微山。
笛奏梅花曲，
刀开明月环。
鼓声鸣海上，
兵气拥云间。
愿斩单于首，
长驱静铁关。

A War Poem

We march forward out of Jade Gate
To fight Huns in the Golden Hills.
A plum tune I play on the flute
And wave my sword with moonlight frills.
The drum sound does the desert quake;
Our morale to the sky does soar.
I would cut off the chieftain's head,
Hence at Iron Pass end the war.

* Jade Gate: an important military fort and passage on the Silk Road, built in the Han dynasty, located in the north of today's Tunhuang, Kansu Province. As is recorded, to guard against Hun invasions, Emperor Martial of Han formed alliance with nations in the western regions to initiate the route between east and west, and instituted four sires and built two passes with beacons west of the Yellow River. Fortresses were made from Lingchü to Wine Spring in 111 B.C. and more fortresses made from Wine Spring to Jade Gate.

* Hun: one of barbaric nomadic Asian peoples who frequently invaded China, a general term referring to all northern or western invaders.
* the Golden Hills: the Altai Mountains, far from the hinterland of China.
* Iron Pass: also known as Irongate Pass, near present-day Korla, New Land (Hsinchiang).

秋　思

春阳如昨日，
碧树鸣黄鹂。
芜然蕙草暮，
飒尔凉风吹。
天秋木叶下，
月冷莎鸡悲。
坐愁群芳歇，
白露凋华滋。

Longing in Autumn

The spring warmth was off yesterday;
On the emerald trees orioles trill.
The orchids wither all too soon;
An autumn wind blows in, so chill.
From the trees dry leaves flutter down;
The moon chills katydids' rue.
She sighs that glamour is all gone,
Plants and grass tinged with hoary dew.

* oriole: golden oriole, one of the family of passerine birds, which looks bright yellow with contrasting black wings and sings beautiful songs.
* orchid: any of a widely distributed family of terrestrial or epiphytic monocotyledonous plants having thickened bulbous roots and often very showy distinctive flowers, one of the four most important floral images in Chinese literature, which are wintersweet, orchid, bamboo, and chrysanthemum.
* katydid: any of several large, green orthopteran insects, having long slender antennae

and long hind legs; the male has highly developed stridulating organs on the forewings, that produce a shrill sound.

* the moon: the celestial body that revolves around the earth from west to east as a satellite, which appears at night and gives off shining silvery light, an image of purity and solitude in Chinese culture.

春　思

燕草如碧丝，
秦桑低绿枝。
当君怀归日，
是妾断肠时。
春风不相识，
何事入罗帷。

Longing in Spring

Yan's grass is thin as silken threads;
Ch'in's mulberries bend their green heads.
When you are in nostalgia drowned,
I've been aching for you, spell-bound.
Shoo, wind, do stay where you should be,
Why blow to my bed to fret me?

* Yan: a northern vassal state of Chough; generally referring to the northern land where soldiers were stationed.
* Ch'in: the first unified regime of China, i.e. the Ch'in Empire.

秋　　思

燕支黄叶落，
妾望自登台。
海上碧云断，
单于秋色来。
胡兵沙塞合，
汉使玉关回。
征客无归日，
空悲蕙草摧。

Longing in Autumn

Atop Mt. Rouge yellow leaves fall;
To look afar, I climb the mound.
O'er the desert no clouds remain;
Ch'anyü comes, autumn hue around.
The news from Jade Gate Pass arrives:
The Hun troops gather and prevail.
My man has no way to come back;
O'er the withered orchids I wail.

* Mt. Rouge: the Rouge Mountains, a range of mountains in today's Ope arms (Changyeh), Kansu Province, lush with pines and cypresses and various kinds of plants and grass, and inhabited by Huns in the Han dynasty.
* Ch'anyü: referring to the chief of a Hun nation.
* Jade Gate Pass: an important military fort and passage on the Silk Road, built in the Han dynasty. It was so named because of the jade business between Han and the western regions.

* Hun: one of barbaric nomadic Asian peoples who frequently invaded China, a general term referring to all northerners or westerners.
* orchid: a terrestrial or epiphytic monocotyledonous plant having thickened bulbous roots and showy distinctive flowers, one of the four most important floral images in Chinese literature, which are wintersweet, orchid, bamboo, and chrysanthemum.

子夜吴歌四首

Wu Tunes by a Girl Called Midnight, Four Poems

春　歌

秦地罗敷女，
采桑绿水边。
素手青条上，
红妆白日鲜。
蚕饥妾欲去，
五马莫留连。

Spring

Lofu, the beauty from Ch'in Land,
Culls mulberry leaves riverside.
The green sprays shade her tender hand,
Her red dress by the bright sun dyed.
"I'd go feed my silkworms", says she,
"Even five horses can't keep me!"

* Lofu: Lofu Ch'in, a belle in the Han dynasty. She showed nice etiquettes even if a prefecture chief flirted with her.
* Ch'in Land: area covered by the first unified regime of China, i.e. the Ch'in Empire.
* mulberry: the edible, berry-like fruit of a tree (genus *Morus*) whose leaves are valued for silkworm culture, and the tree itself, first cultivated in the drainage area of the Yellow River in China about five thousand years ago.
* silkworm: the larva of a moth that produces a dense silken cocoon, especially the common silkworm from whose cocoon commercial silk is made. The silkworm was cultivated in 3000 B.C. when Lace Mum, who was Lord Yellow's concubine, began to raise silkworms and made silk.

夏 歌

镜湖三百里，
菡萏发荷花。
五月西施采，
人看隘若耶。
回舟不待月，
归去越王家。

Summer

Lake Mirror stretches far away;
Lotus lilies blow like a dream.
West Maid, the belle, culls them in May,
The folks spell-bound by the Yeh Stream.
She, not waiting there for the moon,
Rows back to the Lord all too soon.

* Lake Mirror: a large reservoir built in the Han dynasty, higher than the fields and the fields higher than the sea, 310 li in circumference.
* West Maid: once a laundry lady in the State of Yüeh, which was then a tributary to the State of Wu. Because of her beauty, West Maid was selected to be trained in Yüeh's palace, and sent to the King of Wu as a spy. She quickly won the king's affection, making him indulged in her charm. As a result, the State of Wu waned and perished.
* May: the fifth month in Solar calendar or the sixth month in Lunar calendar.
* the moon: the planet of the earth, which appears at night and gives off shining silvery light, an image of purity and solitude in Chinese culture.
* the Yeh Stream: or Joyeh Stream, a stream in the south of present-day Shaohsing, flowing into Lake Mirror. It's said that West Maid did her laundry here.

秋　歌

长安一片月，
万户捣衣声。
秋风吹不尽，
总是玉关情。
何日平胡虏，
良人罢远征。

Autumn

The capital in moonlight drowned,
From each door a pelting sound.
The autumn wind can't blow away
A wife's *Jade Pass*, her sad lay.
"When will our men wipe out the Huns
So they may return, our dear ones?"

* *Jade Pass*: a nostalgic story tracing back to Ch'ao Pan, who garrisoned the border for 31 years and wished he could go back through Jade Pass alive.
* the Huns: nomadic aliens that frequently invaded China.

冬　歌

明朝驿使发，
一夜絮征袍。
素手抽针冷，
那堪把剪刀。
裁缝寄远道，
几日到临洮？

Winter

The courier leaves next morn, as told;
All night a war robe she prepares.
Her fair hand pulls the needle cold;
The cold feel of scissors she bears.
"Will my sewing sent far away
Reach you at Lint'ao with no delay?"

* Lint'ao: one of the fountainheads of the Yellow River culture, an old county established in 384 B.C. during the reign of King Safe of Chough, in present-day Settled West (Tinghsi), Kansu Province.
* my sewing sent far away: an allusion to Chih Ts'ao's lines: I open cask mine to take cloth/And a white silk shirt I will sew.

对 酒 行

松子栖金华,
安期入蓬海。
此人古之仙,
羽化竟何在。
浮生速流电,
倏忽变光彩。
天地无凋换,
容颜有迁改。
对酒不肯饮,
含情欲谁待。

Toasting

Red Pine lived in Mt. Gold Flora,
And Ch'i An on the Fairy Sea.
They are immortals of the past;
Where are they now, where can they be?
A vain life like thunder shoots off;
All too soon, one loses his grace.
Heaven and earth remain the same,
But the human changes his face.
Over the wine sadly I brood;
To drink the cup I have no mood.

* Red Pine: a legendary immortal. It was said that he could regulate winds and rains and burn himself without any harm.

* Mt. Gold Flora: a mountain where Red Pine became immortal, north of what is today's Gold Flora (Chinhua), Chechiang Province.
* Ch'i An: an immortal who had sold medicine at the seaside of East Sea for a thousand years. Emperor First of Ch'in once talked with him for three days. What he talked about was so profound that the emperor could not understand. The emperor gave him a great deal of gold. Ch'i An left the gold at Fuhsiang Pavilion with a letter to ask the emperor to visit him on Fairy Sea a thousand years later.

估 客 行

海客乘天风,
将船远行役。
譬如云中鸟,
一去无踪迹。

Leaving No Trail

Against the wind, on the rough sea,
On business he'll far off sail.
Just like a bird among the clouds,
He vanishes, leaving no trail.

捣 衣 篇

闺里佳人年十馀,
嚬蛾对影恨离居。
忽逢江上春归燕,
衔得云中尺素书。
玉手开缄长叹息,
狂夫犹戍交河北。
万里交河水北流,
愿为双燕泛中洲。
君边云拥青丝骑,
妾处苔生红粉楼。
楼上春风日将歇,
谁能揽镜看愁发?
晓吹筼管随落花,
夜捣戎衣向明月。
明月高高刻漏长,
真珠帘箔掩兰堂。
横垂宝幄同心结,
半拂琼筵苏合香。
琼筵宝幄连枝锦,
灯烛荧荧照孤寝。
有便凭将金剪刀,
为君留下相思枕。
摘尽庭兰不见君,
红巾拭泪生氤氲,
明年若更征边塞,
愿作阳台一段云。

Pestling on Clothes

The boudoir has the beauty in her teens;
She looks at her lone shadow with a frown.
Lo, she sees a swallow over the stream;
With a letter from the clouds it flies down.
She opens the letter and heaves a sigh;
Her man guards the north border as before.
The Link River northbound flows without stop;
Over the shoal there, with him I would soar.
His horse black-maned gallops around the clouds;
Upon her scarlet tower, lo, green moss grows.
The spring wind will go away from her now;
Who'll look into a glass and count her woes?
She plays the tube mid falling blooms at dawn,
And pestles on clothes under the moon bright.
The impearled curtain shades the orchid hall;
The hourglass leaks and leaks to end the night.
A love knot hangs from the mosquito net;
The balm of styrax to the feast does flow.
The feast and tent adorned with entwined twigs,
The lamplight to my bed does faintly glow.
With scissors gold a pillow she will make,
It is for you, a pillow called Love You.
I have picked all orchid flowers in the yard,
And cleaned my tears, but you are not in view.
If you were still on the border next year,
I'd be a cloud above and at you peer.

* swallow: a passerine black bird, with short broad, depressed bill, long pointed wings, and forked tail, noted for fleeting flight and migratory habits. In Chinese culture, swallows are welcome to live with a family with their nest on a beam.
* the Link River: the river flowing around the ancient town called Link River, built by a king of Jushi, in today Turpan, New Land (Hsinchiang), 8,150 li, i.e. 4,075 kilometers from Long Peace, T'ang's capital.
* orchid: a terrestrial or epiphytic monocotyledonous plant, one of the four most important floral images in Chinese literature, which are wintersweet, orchid, bamboo, and chrysanthemum.
* the moon: the celestial body that revolves around the earth from west to east as a satellite, which appears at night and gives off shining silvery light, an image of purity and solitude in Chinese culture.
* hourglass: a vessel used for measuring time by the running of water or sand from the upper into the lower compartment, also used as metaphor for the elapse of time.

少　年　行

君不见
淮南少年游侠客,
白日毬猎夜拥掷。
呼卢百万终不惜,
报仇千里如咫尺。
少年游侠好经过,
浑身装束皆绮罗。
蕙兰相随喧妓女,
风光去处满笙歌。
骄矜自言不可有,
侠士堂中养来久。
好鞍好马乞与人,
十千五千旋沽酒。
赤心用尽为知己,
黄金不惜栽桃李。
桃李栽来几度春,
一回花落一回新。
府县尽为门下客,
王侯皆是平交人。
男儿百年且乐命,
何须徇书受贫病。
男儿百年且荣身,
何须徇节甘风尘。
衣冠半是征战士,
穷儒浪作林泉民。
遮莫枝根长百丈,
不如当代多还往。

遮莫姻亲连帝城，
不如当身自簪缨。
看取富贵眼前者，
何用悠悠身后名。

The Gallant Boy

Don't you espy
The gallant boys from Huainan drift about,
By day hunting, at night casting the die?
For a game, they squander a million away,
To revenge, a thousand miles is just nigh.
The gallant boys just like loafing around,
Fully attired, wearing silk and brocade.
They are surrounded by the balm of belles,
And to enhance them lutes and flutes are played.
They are modest although they look so proud,
Getting along with all those good and fine.
They give their horses and saddles to friends
And spend thousands and thousands on good wine.
With friends they are so generous and stout;
They don't grudge friends any silver or gold.
Friends go away and friends come back again,
New ones they make while sustaining the old.
Magistrates come to pay respect to them;
Marquises are all their equals freewill.
A man is born for pleasure all his life;
Why should he read books while poor and ill?
A man is born for honor and pleasure;
Why should he into a dusty place go?

One should go to the battlefield to fight,
Not like a scholar pacing to and fro.
Do not make use of connections to gain;
You had better do something on your own.
Do not show off your relation with peers;
You can fulfill your purpose all alone.
You should enjoy your wealth before your eye;
Why care about your fame after you die?

* Huainan: an area in the drainage basin of the Huai River, first an eastern barbarian area governed by a vassal state of Chough called Choulai in Western Chough period, enfeoffed as Kingdom of Huainan in the Han dynasty.
* silk: the fine, soft, shiny fiber produced by silk worms to form their cocoons, and the thread or fabric made from this fibre is used as material for clothing. And it can be any clothing made of silk.

长　歌　行

桃李待日开，
荣华照当年。
东风动百物，
草木尽欲言。
枯枝无丑叶，
涸水吐清泉。
大力运天地，
羲和无停鞭。
功名不早著，
竹帛将何宣。
桃李务青春，
谁能贳白日。
富贵与神仙，
蹉跎成两失。
金石犹销铄，
风霜无久质。
畏落日月后，
强欢歌与酒。
秋霜不惜人，
倏忽侵蒲柳。

A Long Song Ballad

Plums and peaches bloom for the day
And adorn the year with their glare.
The east wind each thing has aroused,

Which, it seems, has news to declare.
Bare twigs shoot forth beautiful leaves;
Dried creeks gurgle out springs to slop.
Heaven and earth turn night and day;
She-her drives her cart without stop.
If you don't establish yourself,
How can you carve your name with pride?
Plums and peaches have their best day;
Who can make their glory long bide?
O time and tide wait for no man;
Wealth and God may both go away.
Gold and stone suffer tear and wear;
No dew or frost can for long stay.
I fear time elapses too fast;
So I'm indulged in songs and wine.
When hoarfrost falls down to prevail,
All things fall into a decline.

* She-her: the mother of the sun or the dyad of Goddess of Sun and Goddess of Calendar in Chinese mythology. As is said, She-her, as Goddess of Sun, drives the sun across the sky.
* plums and peaches: an important image in Chinese literature, a metonymy for luxuriance and a metaphor for one's disciples or students.
* God: referring to God's blessings. God, an age-old concept in Chinese culture, identifiable with God in Western culture.

长　相　思

日色已尽花含烟，
月明欲素愁不眠。
赵瑟初停凤凰柱，
蜀琴欲奏鸳鸯弦。
此曲有意无人传，
愿随春风寄燕然。
忆君迢迢隔青天。
昔日横波目，
今成流泪泉。
不信妾肠断，
归来看取明镜前。

Long Longing

The sun setting, the flowers heavy mist hold;
The moon, growing pale, does my woe behold.
The Chao zither has stopped its phoenix lay;
The Shu lute will start its loving bird play.
This song is loving but none can relay;
May spring wind send it to Yanjan today.
I know by the blue sky you're kept away.
Before, you had an angry brow;
Today, you flow into tears now.
If you don't know I'm sad, in plight,
Come back to see me in the mirror bright.

* the moon: the planet of the earth, which appears at night and gives off shining silvery light, an image of purity and solitude in Chinese culture.
* Chao: the State of Chao (403 B.C.- 222 B.C.), a vassal state in the Spring and Autumn period, one of the Seven Powers in the Warring States period.
* Shu: one of the earliest kingdoms in China, founded by Silkworm according to legend. In the Three Kingdoms period, a new Shu was established by Pei Liu, hence one of the three kingdoms in that period.
* lute: a Chinese lute, a stringed musical instrument, played by plucking the strings with fingers or a plectrum.
* Yanjan: Mt. Yanjan, a mountain in today's Mongolia, which is used to refer to the northern land beyond the frontiers.

猛 虎 行

朝作猛虎行,
暮作猛虎吟。
肠断非关陇头水,
泪下不为雍门琴。
旌旗缤纷两河道,
战鼓惊山欲倾倒。
秦人半作燕地囚,
胡马翻衔洛阳草。
一输一失关下兵,
朝降夕叛幽蓟城。
巨鳌未斩海水动,
鱼龙奔走安得宁。
颇似楚汉时,
翻覆无定止。
朝过博浪沙,
暮入淮阴市。
张良未遇韩信贫,
刘项存亡在两臣。
暂到下邳受兵略,
来投漂母作主人。
贤哲栖栖古如此,
今时亦弃青云士。
有策不敢犯龙鳞,
窜身南国避胡尘。
宝书长剑挂高阁,
金鞍骏马散故人。
昨日方为宣城客,

掷铃交通二千石。
有时六博快壮心，
绕床三匝呼一掷。
楚人每道张旭奇，
心藏风云世莫知。
三吴邦伯多顾盼，
四海雄侠皆相推。
萧曹曾作沛中吏，
攀龙附凤当有时。
溧阳酒楼三月春，
杨花漠漠愁杀人。
胡人绿眼吹玉笛，
吴歌白纻飞梁尘。
丈夫相见且为乐，
槌牛挝鼓会众宾。
我从此去钓东海，
得鱼笑寄情相亲。

Tiger Tune

At dawn I compose *Tiger Tune*;
At dusk *Ode to Tiger* I sing.
I do not feel sad because of *Mt. Bulge*,
Nor shed tears because of the sad lute string.
Flags flutter up along the twin rivers;
War drums surprise the mountains falling down.
Ch'in folks are captured by Yan invaders;
Their horses eat grass in Capital Town.
The royal troops retreat to Fisher Gate;
The northern towns are betrayed and give way.

The huge turtle, not yet slayed, heaves the sea;
Officials and folks flee, no peaceful day.
Like the war between Han and Ch'u,
Just forward and back, up and down.
To Breaker Sand I have once been
And also been to Huaishade Town.
Liang Chang lay useless and Hsin Han was poor;
The fate of the nation they could decide.
Chang gained *The Art of War* from Yellow Stone;
Han on Washing Mother's relief relied.
Saints and sages have been treated like this;
And now laid aside are the able ones.
With best ideas, see the Lord I dare not
And flee to the south to evade the Huns.
My saddle and horse are given to friends;
My books and sword are laid by, lying waste.
Yesterday I went to Hsuan as a guest,
And was shown around by the magistrate.
I gambled to vent my indignation;
Around my bed I ran thrice, my arms thrown.
All people in Ch'u say Hsu Chang's a talent;
But his ambition's to the world unknown.
The grandees in Wu hold him in esteem;
To see him all heroes in the world vie.
Hsiao and Ts'ao used to be P'ei's menial clerks;
Once they had the right time, they could fly high.
The third moon, I'd a party in Lishine;
Catkins annoying me were blown in flight.
The Huns growing blue eyes played the jade flute;
The dancing girls from Wu sang *Ramie White*.
We men should make merry when we gather,

Slaughtering bulls, beating drums for the while.
Now, hereby I'd go fishing in East Sea,
And send fish to friends and folks with a smile.

* *Mt. Bulge*: a song in the ancient times, expressing a sense of sorrow and suffering towards a wandering life. Mt. Bulge is a mountain located in the southeast of present-day Kansu Province, 2,928 meters above sea level and about 240 kilometers long from north to south, the borderline between Sha'anhsi Loess Plateau and West Bulge Loess Plateau.
* The twin rivers: implying the first places that fell in Lushan An's Rebellion.
* Ch'in folks: referring to the people living on the central plain.
* Yan: referring to the base of Lushan An's rebel forces.
* the huge turtle: an allusive reference to Lushan An. A soldier of the Kitan race, Lushan An distinguished himself in fighting against his own tribes, and then won the favor of Imperial Consort Yang and the confidence of Emperor Deepire. He was ennobled as a duke, and made the governor of the border provinces of the north, where he held under command the best armies of the empire. In the spring of 755, Lushan An, under the pretext of ridding the court of Premier Kuochung Yang, raised the standard of rebellion. He quickly captured Loshine, occupied the entire territory north of the Yellow River and then devastated Long Peace.
* the war between Han and Ch'u: the war happened in 206 B.C. and lasted for four years, which was a large-scale fight for the throne in the late Ch'in dynasty and ended with Han's victory.
* Huaishade: the birthplace of Hsin Han, a founding commander of Han, in the hinterland of the northern plain of Chiangsu, on the southern bank of the Huai River, hence the name.
* Liang Chang: Liang Chang (250 B.C.- 186 B.C.), a renowned strategist in Chinese history and one of the Three Standouts of the early Han. Once he met an old man at a river, and Chang treated the old man with respect and patience though the old man was arrogant and impolite. After several tests, the old man was finally touched by Chang's sincerity and gave him *The Art of War*, and not until this moment did Chang realize that the old man was Yellow Stone, a legendary Wordist. By studying this book, Liang Chang became a wise and resourceful brain truster.
* Hsin Han: Hsin Han (231 B.C.- 196 B.C.), an outstanding and founding commander of the Han Empire. When he was young, he was not successful in his pursuit of an official career or good at doing business, and he used to rely on an elder laundry

woman who pitied him and gave him food without expectation of rewarding.
* Washing Mother: referring to the laundry lady who provided Hsin Han with food when the later commander was helplessly poor.
* Hsuan: a county instituted in the early years of the Ch'in Emperor under the Prefecture of Redshine. It became a prefecture in 281 during the Chin dynasty. It is well known for rich historical legacies, and best remembered for its high-quality rice paper.
* Ch'u: a vassal state of Chough, one of the powers in the Warring States period, conquered and annexed by Ch'in in 223 B.C., covering the regions of present-day Hunan and Hupei and neighboring areas.
* Hsu Chang: Hsu Chang (A.D. 675 – A.D. 750), a calligrapher in the T'ang dynasty who created a rapid cursive style of writing.
* Wu: an alternative name for the regions south of the Yangtze River.
* Ho Hsiao: Ho Hsiao (257 B.C.- 193 B.C.), a statesman, the first prime minister and one of the Three Standouts in the early Han dynasty.
* Ts'an Ts'ao: a well-known military commander and the second prime minister of Han, namely the prime minster after Ho Hsiao.
* East Sea: what is now East China Sea.

去 妇 词

古来有弃妇,
弃妇有归处。
今日妾辞君,
辞君遣何去。
本家零落尽,
恸哭来时路。
忆昔未嫁君,
闻君却周旋。
绮罗锦绣段,
有赠黄金千。
十五许嫁君,
二十移所天。
自从结发日未几,
离君缅山川。
家家尽欢喜,
孤妾长自怜。
幽闺多怨思,
盛色无十年。
相思若循环,
枕席生流泉。
流泉咽不扫,
独梦关山道。
及此见君归,
君归妾已老。
物情恶衰贱,
新宠方妍好。
掩泪出故房,

伤心剧秋草。
自妾为君妻,
君东妾在西。
罗帏到晓恨,
玉貌一生啼。
自从离别久,
不觉尘埃厚。
尝嫌玳瑁孤,
犹羡鸳鸯偶。
岁华逐霜霰,
贱妾何能久。
寒沼落芙蓉,
秋风散杨柳。
以比憔悴颜,
空持旧物还。
馀生欲何寄,
谁肯相牵攀。
君恩既断绝,
相见何年月。
悔倾连理杯,
虚作同心结。
女萝附青松,
贵欲相依投。
浮萍失绿水,
教作若为流。
不叹君弃妾,
自叹妾缘业。
忆昔初嫁君,
小姑才倚床。
今日妾辞君,
小姑如妾长。

回头语小姑，
莫嫁如兄夫。

A Deserted Wife

Deserted wives there are as e'er;
They've somewhere to go, here or there.
Now to my man I say adieu,
But where, where on earth can I go?
My mother's family's no more;
The way before me I deplore.
Before I was wed to you there,
You were good at social affair.
When I was betrothed, lots of gold
Was paid besides gifts manifold.
At fifteen I was betrothed and
At twenty I was at your hand.
Only a few days I had stayed with you,
To rills and hills you had to go.
All families enjoy their boon;
So wretched, I was left alone.
In great solitude did I stay;
Within ten years I saw decay.
Yearning and turning, I missed you,
On my pillow my tears did flow.
Day and night gurgled the choked stream;
The pass way appeared in my dream.
Now finally, you have come back,
I have grown weak and old, alack.
All dislike something old and low;

All enjoy what is young and new.
In tears drowned, I leave my old room,
Like autumn grass tinted with gloom.
Since I was, as your wife, distressed,
You've lived east and I've been here west.
In bed I stay from grief to spite,
With tears soaking the rosebud bright.
Since you left, I've had tears and wears
And dust has gathered unawares.
A lonely hawksbill I won't be;
Mandarin ducks appeal to me.
Graupel chasing one won't him spare;
How long can I this mishap bear?
Lotuses fall into mud chill;
Willows sway in autumn wind shrill.
My face weary and my skin slack,
With my old dowry I go back.
For my life left, where shall I be?
Who is willing to accept me?
Since your passion does not remain,
Which year can I see you again?
I rue having with you entwined,
And having the same love and mind.
The trailer climbs up the green pine
So to share its valor and shine.
Now the duckweed has lost the blue,
To which place on earth can it flow?
I don't groan you've abandoned me,
Because our cause has ceased to be.
When I was married to you then,
Your little sister was half ten.

Now as I leave here, all alone,
Your sister's as tall as me grown.
To your sister I turn my head:
None like your brother you should wed.

* hawksbill: a tropical marine turtle which furbishes the best grade of tortoise shell used in commerce and collected by rich families as a valuable.
* mandarin ducks: duck-like love birds that always appear in pairs, a metaphor for couples in Chinese culture.
* lotus: one of the various plants of the waterlily family, noted for their large floating leaves and showy flowers, a symbol of purity and elegance in Chinese culture, unsoiled though out of soil, so clean with all leaves green.
* willow: any of a large genus of shrubs and trees related to the poplars, having generally smooth branches, and often long, slender, pliant, and sometimes pendent branchlets, a symbol of farewell, longing or nostalgia in Chinese culture.
* pine: a cone-bearing tree having needle-shaped evergreen leaves growing in clusters, a symbol of longevity and rectitude in Chinese culture.
* duckweed: any of several small, disk-shaped, floating aquatic plants common in streams and ponds.

古近体诗二十八首
Old-new Rhythmic Poetry, 28 Poems

襄　阳　歌

落日欲没岘山西，
倒著接䍦花下迷。
襄阳小儿齐拍手，
拦街争唱《白铜鞮》。
旁人借问笑何事，
笑杀山公醉似泥。
鸬鹚杓，鹦鹉杯。
百年三万六千日，
一日须倾三百杯。
遥看汉水鸭头绿，
恰似葡萄初酦醅。
此江若变作春酒，
垒曲便筑糟丘台。
千金骏马换小妾，
醉坐雕鞍歌《落梅》。
车旁侧挂一壶酒，
凤笙龙管行相催。
咸阳市中叹黄犬，
何如月下倾金罍？
君不见
晋朝羊公一片石，
龟头剥落生莓苔。
泪亦不能为之堕，
心亦不能为之哀。
清风朗月不用一钱买，
玉山自倒非人推。
舒州杓，

力士铛，
李白与尔同死生。
襄王云雨今安在？
江水东流猿夜声。

Song of Sowshine

Beyond the west of Mt. Steep the sun's sunk;
Beneath the flowers I falter down, so drunk.
Patting hands, the kids downtown do me greet,
Singing *White Copper Shoes*, barring the street.
When asked: who on earth are you laughing at?
They point at me: You're boozed, reeling like that.
Cormorant ladle, and parrot handle!
Thirty-six thousand days, a hundred years,
I drink up three hundred cups for three cheers.
Lo, in the Han River green duck heads shine;
Just like grape pulp has mellowed to be wine.
For flowing wine if the Han we could thank,
We'd build a distiller mound on the bank.
Ts'ao changed a concubine for a horse fine;
Astride it, singing *Plums Fall*, drunk with wine.
A kettle hung on the side of his cart,
The flutes and bands did urge him to depart.
"Yellow dog", whined Li, the premier pent-up;
Could he match me drinking my moonlit cup?
Don't you espy
Lord Goat in Chin's Age had a tablet stone,
Whose turtle head did peel off, with moss strewn?
For it, my tears are kept in, not to flow;

My heart, also, will not let out its woe.
Brisk wind or the bright moon you don't have to buy;
When a mount falls; to push you need not try.
Shuchow's spoon you ply,
Giant's Pan you hold high,
Pai Li will stay with you, to live or die.
Where is King Hsiang's mist and rain in his dream?
The river flows east, monkeys' shrieks downstream.

* Mt. Steep: an important fort in history, located in the southwest of Sowshine (Hsiangyang) with the River Han to its east.
* *White Copper Shoes*: an ancient children's song.
* the Han River: the longest branch of the Long River, having an important position in Chinese history.
* green duck heads: a dyeing term referring to a green color similar to that on duck heads. A duck is a web-footed, short-legged, broad-billed water bird of the *Anatidae* family comprising fresh-water and wood ducks.
* concubine: a cohabitant or secondary wife. China was a polygamous society from prehistoric years till the first half of the twentieth century.
* *Plums Fall*: an ancient flute song, one of the twenty eight tunes in Han Conservatoire, first composed by Yennian Li (? - 90 B.C.) in the Western Han dynasty, a eulogy of wintersweets blossoming to brave the cold winter.
* dog: a domesticated carnivorous mammal (*Canis familiaris*), of worldwide distribution and many varities, noted for its adaptability and its devotion to man. The dog was domesticated in China at least 8,000 years ago and used as a hunter, as a poem in *The Book of Songs* says: "The dog bells clink and clink; / The hunter's handsome, a real pink."
* Li: an allusion to Ssu Li (284 B.C.- 208 B.C.), prime minister of Ch'in, a renowned statesman, litterateur and calligrapher, whose political ideas have had a profound impact on China and laid the foundation of China's political system for more than two thousand years. After Emperor First of Ch'in died, Ssu was given a death sentence due to a false accusation. Before the execution, he sighed to his son to be executed with him that it would be impossible to hunt with his yellow dog anymore. This has often been quoted to indicate the sinister risks in the pursuit of a political life.
* Lord Goat: a commander in the Chin dynasty, who garrisoned in Sowshine. He

promoted schooling and won over the trust of the people and the soldiers with nobility. To memorize his achievements, the people in Sowshine set a tablet on Mt. Steep. As the people could not help shedding tears once they saw the tablet, they named it Tablet Tear.

* turtle: referring to a tortoise-like beast in mythology. In China, tablets of great importance were usually carried on the back of a turtle-like creature, which is said to be a figure of the sixth son of the dragon, who is strong and keen on carrying a heavy load.
* Goddess of Mt. Witch: a beautiful fairy dwelling in Mt. Witch, who shaped herself as clouds at dawn and turned into rain at dusk. In myths, King Huai of Ch'u once met her in his dream, and had an intercourse overnight. The story was recorded by Jade Sung, a student of Yüan Ch'ü, when he travelled to Cloud Dream Moor with King Hsiang.

南都行

南都信佳丽，
武阙横西关。
白水真人居，
万商罗鄽闠。
高楼对紫陌，
甲第连青山。
此地多英豪，
邈然不可攀。
陶朱与五羖，
名播天壤间。
丽华秀玉色，
汉女娇朱颜。
清歌遏流云，
艳舞有馀闲。
遨游盛宛洛，
冠盖随风还。
走马红阳城，
呼鹰白河湾。
谁识卧龙客，
长吟愁鬓斑。

South Town

South Town teems with all bells indeed;
The Martial Hills roll from West Pass.
White Water Immortal used to live here;

Businessmen come and go, what a mass!
High towers over the purple streets,
Houses link with hills, roof to roof.
This place boasts so many heroes,
Who're so worthy, vainglory-proof.
Pottery Red and Fifth Black Ram
Are famous between earth and sky.
Lo, the empress called Brilliant Bloom,
And Marsh Maid who made all blooms shy.
Their clarion song stopped flowing clouds;
Their faddish dance stirred many hearts.
Southshine was as rich as Loshine,
Teeming with canopies and carts.
I'm galloping outside Red Sun,
Hunting with my hawk by White Bay.
Who knows me, a crouching dragon,
Crooning, chanting to my hair gray?

* South Town: Southshine, Emperor Lightmight's hometown. As it was south of Loshine, the capital of Eastern Han, it was called South Town, the secondary capital of Eastern Han.
* White Water Immortal: an alternative name for Hsiu Liu, Emperor Lightmight of Han, whose military and political power increased in a place called White Water in South Town.
* Pottery Red: referring to Li Fan (536 B.C.- 448 B.C.), a statesman of Yüeh. He named himself Pottery Red for he lived in Pottery Mound later in his life. Li Fan is one of the earliest mercantile theorists and one of the Five Sages of South Town. Rising from a humble origin, he was erudite and versatile. Discontented with the bureaucracy in Ch'u, he went to assist King of Yüeh to develop the state and wipe out the State of Wu. After he accomplished both success and fame, he changed his name and lived in seclusion.
* Fifth Black Ramp: referring to Hundred Mile Slave, who was exiled to Ch'u after his motherland perished. King Solemn of Ch'in redeemed him with five sheep skins and

appointed him as a senior official.
* Brilliant Bloom: the empress, Hsiu Liu's wife, originally from South Town.
* Marsh Maid: a girl playing with pearls near a river, as recorded in *Ode to South Town* of Heng Chang, one of the Five Sages of South Town.
* Southshine: an old name as well as an alternative name of South Town.
* Loshine: Loyang if transliterated, one of the four ancient capitals in China, along with Long Peace (Hsi'an), Gold Hill (Nanking) and Peking, and it was the second largest city in the T'ang dynasty.
* Red Sun: a county located in South Town.
* crouching dragon: referring to Bright Chuke (A.D. 181 - A.D. 234), a statesman and strategist, prime minister of the Kingdom of Shu in the period of the Three Kingdoms (A.D. 220 - A.D. 265).

江 上 吟

木兰之枻沙棠舟，
玉箫金管坐两头。
美酒樽中置千斛，
载妓随波任去留。
仙人有待乘黄鹤，
海客无心随白鸥。
屈平辞赋悬日月，
楚王台榭空山丘。
兴酣落笔摇五岳，
诗成笑傲凌沧洲。
功名富贵若长在，
汉水亦应西北流。

A Croon on the River

Jade flutes in the front, gold bands in the rear,
Magnolia oars propel the begonia boat.
The wine vessels brimming with mellow wine,
Singers charm me on waves, afloat, afloat.
The saint will go, astride a yellow crane
While I play with white seagulls in the air.
Yüan Chü's lyrics outshine the sun and moon;
King of Ch'u's towers tremble on the hill bare.
In high glee I write to move the five mounts;
The verse finished soars high over the blue.
If titles, wealth and ranks could long remain,

The Han River would back to northwest flow.

* magnolia: any of a genus (*Magnolia*) of trees or shrubs with large, fragrant and usually showy flowers.
* begonia: a plant of a large and widely distributed semitropical genus (*Begonia*) with brilliantly colored leaves and showy irregular flowers.
* seagull: a kind of sea bird, any gull or large tern, a symbol of clean integrity. The seagulls in the Wordist book *Sir Line* (Liehtzu) are particularly sensitive to impurity of motive and will make friends only with the completely guileless and disinterested.
* Yüan Ch'ü: Yüan Ch'ü (340 B.C.- 278 B.C.), a great patriotic poet and a loyal minister of Ch'u, who threw himself into the River Milo, wronged by other aristocrats and so aggrieved at his broken land. He is esteemed as father of Chinese poetry by virtue of being the first named poet of importance and the author of the great and exceptionally long poem *Woebegone*.
* Ch'u: one of the most powerful vassal states of Chough, one of the powers in the Warring States period, conquered and annexed by Ch'in in 223 B.C.
* King of Ch'u's towers: referring to luxurious towers built by King Spirit and King Lush of Ch'u long ago.
* the five mounts: referring to the Five Mountains in China, including Mount Ever in Shanhsi, Mount Scale in Hunan, Mount Arch in Shantung, Mount Flora in Sha'anhsi, and Mount Tower in Honan, which symbolizes the unity of the Chinese nation from north, south, east, west and the central part.
* the Han River: the longest branch of the Long River, having an important position in Chinese history.

侍从宜春苑奉诏赋龙池柳色初青听新莺百啭歌

东风已绿瀛洲草，
紫殿红楼觉春好。
池南柳色半青青，
萦烟袅娜拂绮城。
垂丝百尺挂雕楹，
上有好鸟相和鸣，
间关早得春风情。
春风卷入碧云去，
千门万户皆春声。
是时君王在镐京，
五云垂晖耀紫清。
仗出金宫随日转，
天回玉辇绕花行。
始向蓬莱看舞鹤，
还过茝若听新莺。
新莺飞绕上林苑，
愿入箫韶杂凤笙。

Accompanying His Majesty in Fair Spring Park and Composing a Poem at His Request to Describe the Spring at Dragon Pool While Warblers Sing

The east wind has greened the grass on the isles;
Purple halls and red towers the spring beguiles.

South of the pool willows sway up and down,
And bring half green to stroke the misty town.
Around the carved columns thick catkins fly;
Above them lovely birds each to each cry;
They know the spring has already come by.
To the clouds a spring zephyr whirls and blows;
All households have been tinted with spring hues.
Right now His Majesty's in the hall high,
Auspicious clouds looking down from the sky.
His parade comes out now, swooning the sun;
His carts around the cluster of flowers run.
First they go to Fair Isles to see cranes dance,
And then in Balm Rose hear warblers' romance.
The warblers over High Park chirp a song;
May their singing our happiness prolong.

* Dragon Pool: a pool behind Rise-Laud Palace, so named because auspicious clouds in the shape of a dragon were often seen to hang above.
* purple halls and red towers: referring to royal palaces.
* willow: any of a large genus of shrubs and trees related to the poplars, widely distributed in China and most of the world, having glossy green leaves resembling a girl's eye-brow, and generally having smooth branches, and often long, slender, pliant, and sometimes pendent branchlets, which seem to be waving good-bye, or weeping amorously, or drooping for nostalgia.
* catkin: a deciduous scaly spike of flowers, as in the willow, an image of helpless drifting or wandering in Chinese literature.
* Fair Isles: also known as Mt. Fairyland or Fairyland, three fairy isles held up by giant turtles in East Sea, a dwelling place of immotals and exalted spirits, regarded as today's P'englai Isles governed by Shantung Province.
* Balm Rose: a royal hall in a Han palace.
* High Park: an imperial park that Lord Martial of Han built on the site of a discarded park of Ch'in. It was vast and splendid with palaces and woodlands, having various functions and recreational facilities, rolling about 340 kilometers.

玉 壶 吟

烈士击玉壶，
壮心惜暮年。
三杯拂剑舞秋月，
忽然高咏涕泗涟。
凤凰初下紫泥诏，
谒帝称觞登御筵。
揄扬九重万乘主，
谑浪赤墀青琐贤。
朝天数换飞龙马，
敕赐珊瑚白玉鞭。
世人不识东方朔，
大隐金门是谪仙。
西施宜笑复宜嚬，
丑女效之徒累身。
君王虽爱蛾眉好，
无奈宫中妒杀人！

A Song of the Jade Pot

The gallant the jade pot did beat,
Sighing: Time to old age does fleet.
Drinking cups, I play my sword to the moon,
And my tears flow while a sad song I croon.
When I receive the edict from the crown,
To the grand imperial feast I am shown.
The Most High I sing praise of and revere;

The courtiers I meet on the step and jeer.
　　I am granted great horses to run fast,
　　And blessed with a golden whip to go past.
　　Newmoon East people do not know at all;
　　Like him, I, a recluse, hide in the hall.
　　Like West Maid I'm favored for my sweet smile;
　　They, like the miming ugly, lose their style.
　　Though His Majesty is fond of my charm,
　　The jealous courtiers have brought me much harm.

* jade pot: a pot usually alluding to the purity of the holder's heart, and sometimes referring to the pure world of immortality, where elixirs are concocted.
* the moon: the celestial body that revolves around the earth from west to east as a satellite, which appears at night and gives off shining silvery light, an image of purity and solitude in Chinese culture.
* edict: a public ordinance emanating from a sovereign and having the force of law.
* Newmoon East: referring to Shuo Tungfang (154 B.C.- 93 B.C.), a jocular and witted official serving Emperor Martial of Han.
* West Maid: once a laundry lady in the State of Yüeh, which was then a tributary to the State of Wu. Because of her beauty, West Maid was selected to be trained in Yüeh's palace, and sent to the King of Wu as a spy. She quickly won the king's affection, making him indulged in her charm. As a result, the State of Wu waned and perished.

豳歌行上新平长史兄粲

豳谷稍稍振庭柯，
泾水浩浩扬湍波。
哀鸿酸嘶暮声急，
愁云苍惨寒气多。
忆昨去家此为客，
荷花初红柳条碧。
中宵出饮三百杯，
明朝归揖二千石。
宁知流寓变光辉，
胡霜萧飒绕客衣。
寒灰寂寞凭谁暖，
落叶飘扬何处归。
吾兄行乐穷曛旭，
满堂有美颜如玉。
赵女长歌入彩云，
燕姬醉舞娇红烛。
狐裘兽炭酌流霞，
壮士悲吟宁见嗟。
前荣后枯相翻覆，
何惜馀光及棣华。

A Pin Song, to My Cousin Ts'an, Vice Prefect

In the State of Pin from trees drop leaves dried;
The Ching River sees its water push a tide.

The sad wild geese at nightfall shriek and shrill;
The worried clouds drift thru so much pale chill.
Since he left his homeland, here he has been;
The lotuses bloom and willows sway green.
I've drunk three hundred cups of wine at noon;
I will say farewell to the prefect soon.
Who knows time flies and it flies so fast now;
Hoarfrost tints my clothes in an autumn sough.
Solitary, where can one in warmth stay?
And where can the leaf rest now blown astray?
My cousin, you seek pleasure day and night,
With girls swarming in your hall, beaming bright.
The maids sing a song that rings in the air;
The belles dance a dance to the candle glare.
In fox fur and by charcoal he drinks wine;
A true hero will sing aloud, not whine.
Things flourish and fade in turn without end;
As e'er, siblings should on siblings depend.

* The State of Pin: an ancient state established by ancestors of the Chough House.
* the Ching River: the largest branch of the Yellow River, originating from Kansu and flowing into the Yellow River in Sha'anhsi, and also a branch of the Wei River originating from Ninghsia.
* wild goose: an undomesticated goose that is caring and responsible, taken as a symbol of benevolence, righteousness, good manner, wisdom, and faith in Chinese culture.
* lotus: one of the various plants of the waterlily family, noted for their large floating leaves and showy flowers, a symbol of purity and elegance in Chinese culture, unsoiled though out of soil, so clean with all leaves green.
* willow: a symbol of farewell in Chinese culture. The best image is in *Vetch We Pick*, a verse in *The Book of Songs*, which is like this: When we left long ago, / The willows waved adieu. / Now back to our home town, / We meet snow falling down.
* candle: a cylinder of tallow, wax, or other solid fat, containing a wick, to give light when burning, first seen in literature in the Eastern Han dynasty. The most famous

lines about candles are from a poem by a T'ang poet named Shangyin Li, "Silkworms stop offering silk when they die; / Candles become ash as their tears run dry."

* fox: a burrowing canine mammal (genus *Vulpes*) having a long pointed muzzle and a long bushy tail, commonly reddish-brown in color, characterized by its cunning.

西岳云台歌送丹丘子

西岳峥嵘何壮哉！
黄河如丝天际来。
黄河万里触山动，
盘涡毂转秦地雷。
荣光休气纷五彩，
千年一清圣人在。
巨灵咆哮擘两山，
洪波喷箭射东海。
三峰却立如欲摧，
翠崖丹谷高掌开。
白帝金精运元气，
石作莲花云作台。
云台阁道连窈冥，
中有不死丹丘生。
明星玉女备洒扫，
麻姑搔背指爪轻。
我皇手把天地户，
丹丘谈天与天语。
九重出入生光辉，
东来蓬莱复西归。
玉浆倘惠故人饮，
骑二茅龙上天飞。

A Song to Redknoll at Cloud Mound of Mt. Flora

Mt. Flora, west there, how it towers, how high;

The Yellow River like silk runs from the sky.
Ten thousand miles long, all mountains it shakes;
With whirlpools rumbling, the Ch'in Land it quakes.
The sun, the foams, and the resplendent glow;
A saint purges its ten thousand years' flow.
Like a giant spirit, mountains it cuts through;
With tumbling waves it shoots to the east blue.
The three peaks cower back, giving in to harm,
The cliffs, the vales, the print of a huge palm.
White God has its essences finely ground
To make stone lotuses and a cloud mound.
The cloud mound with a stack pass links the sky,
Where Redknoll, an immortal, will not die.
Bright Star and Jade clean for him without fail;
Hemp Girl titillates him with her light nail.
Mother West keeps the gate to sky and earth;
Redknoll talks about the Word and its worth.
He goes thru the space with all glamours blessed,
Comes to Fairyland and then returns west.
Nectar if I could drink with my good friend,
We'd ride thatch dragons and the sky ascend.

* Redknoll: a Wordist adept, Pai Li's friend. It was he who recommended Pai Li for a position in the capital.
* Cloud Mound: a peak of Mt. Flora, one of the five sacred mountains in ancient China.
* Mt. Flora: one of the Sacred Five Mountains in China, representing the west, regarded as the steepest and saintly mountain in China as it is one of the progenitors of Chinese culture, the shrine of Wordism and the abode of God of Mt. Flora, located in today's Flowershade, Sha'anhsi Province.
* Ch'in: the Ch'in State or the State of Ch'in (905 B.C.- 206 B.C.), one of the most powerful vassal states in the Chough dynasty, which developed into the first unified regime of China, i.e. the Ch'in Empire.

* A saint purges its ten thousand years' flow: Ancient Chinese regarded it as an implication of a clean governance if the Yellow River appeared clean.
* a giant spirit: referring to a river spirit. It was said that there was only one peak on Mt. Flora in ancient times, and a giant spirit cut the mountain into halves with his bare hands, so that the river rushed directly through the mountains.
* the three peaks: referring to the three peaks on Mt. Flora, including Sun Greeting Peak in the east, Wild Geese Peak in the south, and Lotus Peak in the west.
* White God: the god in charge of the west, one of the five heavenly lords in Chinese mythology.
* Bright Star and Jade: fairies living on Mt. Flora.
* Hemp Girl: an alternative name of Maid Flax, a mythical figure, who looks eighteen years old but claims to have witnessed the drying of East Sea for three times.
* Mother West: a sovereign goddess living on Mt. Queen in Chinese myths, regarded as a goddess in charge of women protection, marriage and procreation, and longevity. Her appearance was originally described as human-bodied, tiger-toothed, leopard-tailed and hoopoe-haired.
* the Word: referring to Tao if transliterated, the most significant and profoundest concept in Chinese philosophy. According to Laocius's *The Word and the World*: "The Word is void, but its use is infinite. O deep! It seems to be the root of all things."
* Fiaryland: a fabled floating island supported by giant turtles in East Sea, a dwelling place of exalted spirits and Wordist immortals.
* thatch dragon: a fabulous serpent-like giant winged animal that an immortal rode to the sky. According to a fable, a sorcerer called Sir First in Mid-Han, when dying at more than a hundred years old, asked the tavern owner's wife to dress up and go with him to enter a mausoleum. On that night two immortals came each riding a thatch dog to pick up Sir First. Sir First offered one to the wife and kept one for himself. The thatch dogs changed into thatch dragons while flying to Mt. Flora.

元丹丘歌

元丹丘，爱神仙，
朝饮颍川之清流，
暮还嵩岑之紫烟，
三十六峰长周旋。
长周旋，蹑星虹，
身骑飞龙耳生风，
横河跨海与天通，
我知尔游心无穷。

A Song to Redknoll

Lo, Redknoll, my friend, immortals he loves.
At dawn, from the stream he drinks a clear flow.
At dusk, he returns to Mt. Tower mid clouds,
And round Thirty-six Peaks go high and low.
Going high and low, the rainbow sky-bound,
He rides a dragon with a whirling sound.
Across rivers and seas, up to the sky,
He'll soar far and high, I know, without bound.

* Redknoll: a Wordist adept and an important friend of Pai Li's. Pai Li met him at the age of twenty and once lived in seclusion with him on Mt. Tower. With their twenty-four years' friendship and correspondence, Rendknoll exerted great influence on Pai Li, who wrote 14 poems dedicated to the former.
* Mt. Tower: one of the Five Mountains in China, which lies in the centre while the other four are located in different directions. It is one of the five sanctuaries of Wordism, and the abode of God of Mt. Tower worshipped by Han Chinese, with an

area of 450 square kilometers, consisting of Mt. Greatroom and Mt. Smallroom, having 72 peaks, 350 meters above sea level at the lowest and 1,512 meters at the highest.

* Thirty-six Peaks: There are thirty-six peaks on one of the mountains of Mt. Tower, i.e., Mt. Smallroom.
* He rides a dragon with a whirling sound: In Wordism, riding a dragon is usually a sign of being immortal.
* dragon: a fabulous serpent-like giant winged animal, a symbol of benevolence and sovereignty in Chinese culture.

扶风豪士歌

洛阳三月飞胡沙,
洛阳城中人怨嗟。
天津流水波赤血,
白骨相撑如乱麻。
我亦东奔向吴国,
浮云四塞道路赊。
东方日出啼早鸦,
城门人开扫落花。
梧桐杨柳拂金井,
来醉扶风豪士家。
扶风豪士天下奇,
意气相倾山可移。
作人不倚将军势,
饮酒岂顾尚书期。
雕盘绮食会众客,
吴歌赵舞香风吹。
原尝春陵六国时,
开心写意君所知。
堂中各有三千士,
明日报恩知是谁?
抚长剑,一扬眉,
清水白石何离离。
脱吾帽,向君笑;
饮君酒,为君吟。
张良未逐赤松去,
桥边黄石知我心。

A Song of the Gallant

The third moon, Hun sand flies in Loshine Town;
The folks in the town all in sadness drown.
Heaven Ford sees the water with blood flow;
White bones propping up add up to the throe.
To the Wu State I rush, with pains I bear,
Clouds floating high above, all roads stopped there.
The sun rising east, crows cawing to weep,
The gate keeper of the town does blooms sweep.
Parasol trees turn green and catkins fly;
In the gallant's house I would drink till high.
The gallant's so rare in the human world;
He can topple mountains, as far off hurled.
He does not lean on generals' power great;
He does not care if ministers are late.
He treats his friends and guests well, plate and dish;
Lo, songs and dances bring about a wish.
The Age of the Six States you may recall;
So blessed I am, do you know this at all?
In the hall he's three thousand with him stay;
Who knows one day someone may him repay.
Drawing my long sword, I raise my high brow;
How the stream flows on pebbles in a sough!
I take off my hat, and to him I grin;
Your wine I drink up, and your smile I win.
Not for Liang Chang but Red Pine I depart;
Yellow Stone by the bridge does know my heart.

* Loshine Town: Loyang if transliterated, one of the four ancient capitals in China, along with Long Peace (Hsi'an), Gold Hill (Nanking) and Peking, and it was the second largest city in the T'ang dynasty.
* Heaven Ford: a bridge over the River Lo in the southwest of Loshine. In A.D. 755, Lushan An's rebellion forces attacked Loshine and committed innumerable murders.
* parasol tree: Chinese parasol tree, a common tree in China and most of the world, a noble tree where phoenixes perch according to Chinese mythology.
* catkin: a deciduous scaly spike of flowers, as in the willow, an image of helpless drifting or wandering in Chinese literature.
* The Six States: referring to the powerful vassal states under Chough apart from Ch'in, namely Ch'i, Ch'u, Yan, Han, Chao, and Way, which were finally annexed by Ch'in through bribery and war.
* Liang Chang: Liang Chang (250 B.C.- 186 B.C.), a renowned strategist in Chinese history and one of the Three Standouts of the early Han. Polite and respectful, he won the legendary Wordist Yellow Stone's trust and received *The Art of War* from him. By studying the book, Liang Chang became a resourceful brain truster. After the reign of Han was established, he asked for retirement and followed Red Pine to be an immortal. The poet takes Liang Chang as a symbolic figure of his own to imply his own talent and ambition.
* Red Pine: a legendary immortal. It was said that he could regulate winds and rains and burn himself without inflicting harm upon himself.
* Yellow Stone: a legendary Wordist who gave Liang Chang *The Art of War*, which played a decisive part in the latter's life.

同族弟金城尉叔卿烛照山水壁画歌

高堂粉壁图蓬瀛,
烛前一见沧洲清。
洪波汹涌山峥嵘,
皎若丹丘隔海望赤城。
光中乍喜岚气灭,
谓逢山阴晴后雪。
回溪碧流寂无喧,
又如秦人月下窥花源。
了然不觉清心魂,
只将叠嶂鸣秋猿。
与君对此欢未歇,
放歌行吟达明发。
却顾海客扬云帆,
便欲因之向溟渤。

Looking at a Scroll with a Candle with My Cousin, a Constable

A scroll of Fairyland on the white wall;
The candlelit green shoal gives one a call.
By the high mountain waves roll up and down;
The Red Knoll gleaming, one can look thru the sea to Red Town.
The vapour gone out, left is the pure glow,
Like the shady mountainside holding snow.
The creek flowing round, so calm it appears,
Like a Ch'in folk that in the moonlight to Shangrila peers.

This scroll so refreshing, I'm purified,
As if monkeys cry on the mountainside.
Compared with you, I'm in happiness loud;
Till daybreak I chant and sing in mood proud.
Looking back at the sails on the broad sea,
I would go out, a free recluse to be.

* Fairyland: an ideal abode for immortals, sometimes thought of as being in the middle of East Sea, sometimes in the sky.
* Red Knoll: a place immortals dwell.
* Red Town: Mt. Red Town, a mountain located in present-day Shaohsing (Chechiang Province), named because of the red soil covering the land.
* Ch'in: the Ch'in State or the State of Ch'in (905 B.C.- 206 B.C.), one of the most powerful vassal states in the Chough dynasty, which developed into the first unified regime of China, i.e. the Ch'in Empire.

白 毫 子 歌

淮南小山白毫子，
乃在淮南小山里。
夜卧松下云，
朝餐石中髓。
小山连绵向江开，
碧峰巉岩绿水回。
余配白毫子，
独酌流霞杯。
拂花弄琴坐青苔，
绿萝树下春风来。
南窗萧飒松声起，
凭崖一听清心耳。
可得见，未得亲。
八公携手五云去，
空馀桂树愁杀人。

A Song of White Frills

In the Little Huainan Hills lives White Frills;
He still lives in the little Huainan Hills.
At night he sleeps beneath the pine;
At dawn he eats pith of stone spine.
The small hills extend to the river there;
Peaks green, cliffs steep, there winds the water clear.
I can match him, my friend White Frills,
Who alone godly nectar swills.

I sit still under the green apple trees;

From the moss to my lute blows a spring breeze.

To the southern window blows a pine whiff,

Which cleanses my heart and ears by the cliff.

That thing I can see; but it's beyond me.

Hand in hand, Eight Hermits fly to the sky,

Leaving the laurel alone that does sigh.

* White Frills: a legendary hermit in the Han dynasty.
* Little Huainan Hills: referring to a group of people serving as hangers-on of Lord Huainan of Han. The Little Huainan Hills in the next line refers to where White Frills dwelt.
* moss: a tiny, delicate green bryophytic plant growing on damp decaying wood, wet ground, humid rocks or trees, producing capsules which open by an operculum and contain spores. Under a poet's writing brush, it may arouse a poetic feeling or imagination.
* Eight Hermits: hangers-on serving Lord Huainan for his virtue. They became immortals in legends of later generations.
* laurel: an evergreen shrub with aromatic, lance-shaped leaves, yellowish flowers, and succulent, cherry-like fruit, a symbol of glory usually in the form of a crown or wreath of laurel to indicate honor or high merit, especially when one had passed Grand Test, i.e. Civil Service Examinations for selecting government officials, in ancient China.

梁 园 吟

我浮黄河去京阙,
挂席欲进波连山。
天长水阔厌远涉,
访古始及平台间。
平台为客忧思多,
对酒遂作梁园歌。
却忆蓬池阮公咏,
因吟渌水扬洪波。
洪波浩荡迷旧国,
路远西归安可得!
人生达命岂暇愁,
且饮美酒登高楼。
平头奴子摇大扇,
五月不热疑清秋。
玉盘杨梅为君设,
吴盐如花皎白雪。
持盐把酒但饮之,
莫学夷齐事高洁。
昔人豪贵信陵君,
今人耕种信陵坟。
荒城虚照碧山月,
古木尽入苍梧云。
梁王宫阙今安在?
枚马先归不相待。
舞影歌声散绿池,
空馀汴水东流海。
沉吟此事泪满衣,

黄金买醉未能归。
连呼五白行六博,
分曹赌酒酣驰晖。
歌且谣,意方远。
东山高卧时起来,
欲济苍生未应晚。

A Song of Liang's Garden

Cruising the Yellow, Capital I leave;
The sail's hung, the river like hills does heave.
The trip long, the water rolls forward bound;
At last, I reach the ruins of Even Mound.
On Even Mound I'm still sad, prone to whine;
Hence my song of Liang's Park before the wine.
And on Lotus Pond I croon Chi Juan's song,
With the verse of "The waves surging along".
The waves bar the way to Capital there;
Could I e'er go west, over there? Ne'er e'er.
One's fate is arranged, no room for despairs;
Let's just drink our good wine and go upstairs.
The short-haired servant waves a fan for me;
The fifth moon it's not hot, like autumn be.
The plate of plums is well prepared for you;
The Wu salt is so white, just like white snow.
While you may enjoy your salt and your wine;
Don't, like Bow and Straight, try to stay divine.
There was a noble and holy man then;
Now his tomb's being tilled by other men.
Lo, the ruins are lit up by the moon pale;

The old tree stand to reach where clouds prevail.
Where is King of Liang's palace, where's the gate?
Ch'eng Mei and Ssuma don't for others wait.
The dances and songs are gone, here no more;
The Pian River to the east sea does pour.
I croon till my tears soak my clothes, alack;
I buy wine and get drunk, but can't go back.
I call it white, I call it black, and play,
Drinking, gambling just to kick off the day.
I sing out a song; I do strive for long.
On East Mount I sit, I sleep, and I wait;
To help the human world it's ne'er too late.

* Even Mound: a mound built by a prime minister of Sung during the Spring and Autumn period. But the construction was carried out in a farming season, which aroused complaints among the people.
* Liang's Park: also called Prince Liang's Park, a royal park established by Prince Piety of Liang in the Western Han dynasty, located in the ruins of the State of Sung, that is, today's Shangch'iu, Honan Province, the birthplace of Sir Lush, one of the forerunners of Wordism.
* Chi Juan: Chi Juan (A.D. 210 – A.D. 263), a poet of the Three Kingdoms period and one of the Seven Sages of the Bamboo Grove.
* Bow and Straight: referring to Bowone and Straightthree, childes in the late Shang dynasty. As they failed to admonish King Martial of Chough, they left King Chough and refused to take crops planted under the reign of Chough. They lived on fungi on Mt. Firstshine and starved to death in the end.
* his tomb: referring to the tomb of Faith Hill, a prince of Way, who was one of the four noble princes in the Warring States period. Being courteous to men of talents, he attracted 3,000 hangers-on. Faith Hill was admired by his people in Liang (the capital of Way) and appreciated by Pang Liu (the founding emperor of Han). When Pang Liu was enthroned, he arranged five families to guard the tomb of Faith Hill.
* Ch'eng Mei: Ch'eng Mei (? – 140 B.C.), a verse writer in the Western Han dynasty. He often visited Liang's Garden with friends after he declined his position, ill as his excuse.

* Hsiangju Ssuma: Hsiangju Ssuma (179 B.C.- 118 B.C.), a representative prose and verse writer in the Han dynasty. He made acquaintance with Prince Liang of Han, and one of his hangers-on was Ch'eng Mei when King Liang came to the capital to strive for the throne. Not long after King Liang failed, Ssuma resigned and went to live in Liang's Garden, a great park that rolled a hundred miles in circumference.
* The Pian River: an ancient river that originated from Hsingshine and flowed into the Ssu River in P'eng.
* East Mound: the place where An Hsieh (A.D. 320 – A.D. 385) lived. An Hsieh, a statesman and litterateur with a high reputation, lived on East Mound with ease and kept declining official positions.

鸣皋歌送岑徵君

若有人兮思鸣皋，
阻积雪兮心烦劳。
洪河凌兢不可以径度，
冰龙鳞兮难容舠。
邈仙山之峻极兮，
闻天籁之嘈嘈。
霜崖缟皓以合沓兮，
若长风扇海涌沧溟之波涛。
玄猿绿罴，
舔䑛崟危；
咆柯振石，
骇胆栗魄，群呼而相号。
峰峥嵘以路绝，
挂星辰于崖嶅！
送君之归兮，
动鸣皋之新作。
交鼓吹兮弹丝，
觞清泠之池阁。
君不行兮何待？
若返顾之黄鹤。
扫梁园之群英，
振大雅于东洛。
巾征轩兮历阻折，
寻幽居兮越巇崿。
盘白石兮坐素月，
琴松风兮寂万壑。
望不见兮心氛氲，

萝冥冥兮霰纷纷。
水横洞以下渌,
波小声而上闻。
虎啸谷而生风,
龙藏溪而吐云。
冥鹤清唳,
饥鼯嘶呻。
块独处此幽默兮,
愀空山而愁人。
鸡聚族以争食,
凤孤飞而无邻。
蝘蜓嘲龙,
鱼目混珍;
嫫母衣锦,
西施负薪。
若使巢由桎梏于轩冕兮,
亦奚异于夔龙蹩于风尘!
哭何苦而救楚,
笑何夸而却秦?
吾诚不能学二子沽名矫节以耀世兮,
固将弃天地而遗身!
白鸥兮飞来,
长与君兮相亲。

A Song of Swamp to Ts'en the Recruit

Someone like Ts'en for Swamp does aspire;
Barred by heavy snow, o his heart does tire.
The river he can't cross, with ice afloat;
Ice rugged like dragon scales, he can't boat.

The mountain's too steep to climb, clouds adrift;
The clouds resound the whir of wind so swift.
The snow-capped cliffs line up and like haze merge,
Like a great sea is blown up by a long wind to surge.
Monkeys black or bears brown
Frightened there, show their tongue.
Rotten trees tall, shaky rocks high,
So frightening and scaring that all run to cry.
The peaks towering, there's no way out;
The stars are hung on the cliff snout.
Now I see you depart;
To you *Swamp* I'll impart.
To pluck the strings I have now come
And at the feast, I beat the drum.
Why don't you go, why here remain?
Are you waiting for a yellow crane?
Will you all the talents employ?
Will you *The Psalms Major* enjoy?
Your bravery you'll show and your cart you'll ride;
The mountains you'll climb and in caves you'll hide.
Sitting on a rock, you'll see the moon pale;
Hearing wind blowing, you'll live in the dale.
As I can't see you, so I am perturbed;
The pine trailers dim, graupel is disturbed.
A spring through a cave, the water clear;
The ripples murmur and you can them hear.
Tigers roar and with the puff of wind rave;
Dragons spurt out clouds, hiding in the cave.
The cranes in the dark trill;
The bats, so hungry, shrill.
O living alone in this place so chill,

Feeling sad before the vacant hill.

A chicken finds a flock where to vie;

A phoenix does in solitude fly.

Lizards at dragons jeer;

Pearls blend with fish eyes mere.

The ugly wears brocade;

West Maid is a slave made.

Isn't it the case sages like Nest and freedom are jailed?

Isn't it the case talents like Onefoot and Dragon are flailed?

Shen so cried that Ch'u could at last win;

Lu so laughed that he did dispel Ch'in.

But I cannot learn from these two men to fish for fame;

I would sacrifice all to fulfil my aim.

Fly to me, o white crane;

Close to you I will remain.

* Swamp: an attraction to litterateurs, located in present-day Honan Province.
* Ts'en: referring to Ts'en Hsun, Pai Li's friend, also mentioned in Pai Li's *Do Drink Wine*.
* the ugly: referring to Lord Yellow's fourth concubine. She was chosen for her virtue instead of her appearance.
* *The Psalms Major*: one part of *The Book of Songs*, an early collection of Chinese poems including folk songs, psalms and odes.
* tiger: a large carnivorous feline mammal of Asia, with vertical black wavy stripes on a tawny body and black bars or rings on the limbs and tail, praised as king of all animals.
* dragon: a fabulous serpent-like giant winged animal, a symbol of benevolence and sovereignty in Chinese culture.
* lizard: any of various reptiles, as an agama, basilisk, chameleon, geko, glass snake, horned toad, iguana, monitor, or skink.
* pearl: a lustrous, calcareous concretion deposited in layers around a central nucleus in the shells of various mollusks, and largely used as a gem or regarded as a treasure.
* fish eye: a metaphor for something cheap or fake, especially when collocated with "pearl", for example, "pass fish eyes for pearls" means "mix the genuine with the fake".

* West Maid: one of the Four Belles in ancient China. West Maid was a laundry lady of the State of Yüeh, which was then a tributary to State of Wu. Because of her beauty, she was selected to be trained in Yüeh's palace, and sent to King of Wu as a spy. She quickly won the king's affection, making him indulged in her charm. As a result, the State of Wu waned and perished.
* Nest and Freedom: referring to Fu Ch'ao and Yu Hsu. They were both hermits of talent and declined to be king when Mound intended to abdicate the throne to them.
* Onefoot: a mythical creature which looks like a one-legged ox without horns. It comes with a storm and roars like thunder. It is said that Lord Yellow used its skin to make drums and bone to make drumsticks, and the sound could shake the world.
* Shen: referring to Paohsu Shen, a senior official of Ch'u, who cried for help at the city wall of Ch'in for seven days after his motherland perished. His persistence finally moved King of Ch'in to send troops to restore Ch'u. After Ch'u was stabilized, he declined awards and lived in seclusion with his family.
* Chunglien Lu: a political strategist, a sophist. He once helped Lord Plain of Chao successfully persuade the State of Way to fight together against Ch'in. After that, he declined the awards given by Lord Plain and went away.
* Ch'u: a vassal state of Chough, one of the powers in the Warring States period, conquered and annexed by Ch'in in 223 B.C.
* Ch'in: the Ch'in State or the State of Ch'in (905 B.C.- 206 B.C.), one of the most powerful vassal states in the Chough dynasty, which developed into the first unified regime of China, i.e., the Ch'in Empire.

鸣皋歌奉饯从翁清归五崖山居

忆昨鸣皋梦里还,
手弄素月清潭间。
觉时枕席非碧山,
侧身西望阻秦关。
麒麟阁上春还早,
著书却忆伊阳好。
青松来风吹古道,
绿萝飞花覆烟草。
我家仙翁爱清真,
才雄草圣凌古人,
欲卧鸣皋绝世尘。
鸣皋微茫在何处?
五崖峡水横樵路。
身披翠云裘,
袖拂紫烟去。
去时应过嵩少间,
相思为折三花树。

A Song of Swamp at a Farewell Dinner for Uncle Ch'ing Back to Mt. Five Cliffs

Last night I returned to Swamp in my dream;
I stroked Luna that played her shade downstream.
I woke and found my pillow not the hill;
It's barred in the west by Ch'in Pass chill.
Spring has come early to Unicorn Tower;

I'd better stop writing to play an hour.
A sough from the pines blows the olden pass,
Green trailers, flying petals, misty grass!
I, an immortal, love nature and truth;
E'en the grass outshines all, a holy growth.
I'd live in the swamp, of worldly dust free,
But where is the swamp and where can it be?
The woodcutter pass does in gorge flood drown;
Donning an emerald cloud gown,
My sleeve shooing mist, I go down.
Go down! I will pass Mt. Tower on the way;
To muse there, I will break a three-flower spray.

* Swamp: an attraction to litterateurs, located in present-day Honan Province.
* Luna: the goddess of the moon and of months in Roman mythology, and in Chinese culture the imperial concubine of Lord Alarm (2480 B.C.- 2345 B.C.), one of five mythical emperors in prehistorical China. Luna or the moon is an important image in Chinese literature as it can give rise to many associations such as solitude, purity, brightness and happy reunions.
* Ch'in Pass: referring to Case Dale or the land west of Case Dale.
* Unicorn Tower: or Unicorn Mound built in the Han dynasty to memorize those who had made great contributions to the empire.
* Mt. Tower: one of the Five Mountains in China, which lies in the centre among the five, in present-day Honan Province. It is one of the five sanctuaries of Wordism, and the abode of God of Mt. Tower worshipped by Han Chinese, with an area of 450 square kilometers, consisting of Mt. Greatroom and Mt. Smallroom, having 72 peaks, 350 meters above sea level at the lowest and 1512 meters at the highest.
* three-flower spray: a spray from a three-flower tree, i.e., tallipot that flowers three times a year.

劳 劳 亭 歌

金陵劳劳送客堂，
蔓草离离生道旁。
古情不尽东流水，
此地悲风愁白杨。
我乘素舸同康乐，
朗咏清川飞夜霜。
昔闻牛渚吟五章，
今来何谢袁家郎。
苦竹寒声动秋月，
独宿空帘归梦长。

A Song of Farewell Bower

South of the Gold Hills is a farewell bower;
By the road grass grows luxuriant to flower.
For my farewell, the river eastward flows;
To my sorrow, the wind thru poplars blows.
Like Hsieh, Lord Glee, I will take a big boat;
In the frosty night *A Clear Stream* I throat.
I hear Yüan wrote a verse at Ox Shoal there;
But with this talent I could well compare!
An autumn sough stirs the moonlit bamboo;
I sail through my dream, alone on the blue.

* the Gold Hills: what is today's the Rosegold Hills, in today's Nanking, whose alias is Gold Hill.

* Hsieh: referring to Lingyün Hsieh (A.D. 385 – A.D. 433), a Buddhist and traveler in the Northern and Southern dynasties, and a representative topographical poet in Chinese history.
* poplar: any of a genus (*Populus*) of dioecious trees and bushes of the willow family, widely distributed in the northern hemisphere.
* Lord Glee: the court title of Lingyün Hsieh, a poet and famous mountain climber, who invented special mountain shoes.
* Yüan: referring to Hung Yüan (A.D. 328 – 376 A.D.): a metaphysician, litterateur, and historian in the Eastern Chin dynasty. He once amazed the chief of Ox Shoal by a verse he wrote, and achieved fame accordingly.
* Ox Shoal: in today's Maanshan, Anhui Province.

横江词六首
The Heng River, Six Poems

其 一

人道横江好，
侬道横江恶。
一风三日吹倒山，
白浪高于瓦官阁。

No. 1

Someone says the Heng River's good;
"It's bad", while so saying, you cower.
Topple Mt. Heaven Gate the strong wind would;
The white waves fly higher than the temple tower.

* the Heng River: in present-day Anhui Province.
* Mt. Heaven Gate: many mountains in China bearing this name, most probably the one in Wuhu, Anhui Province.

其 二

海潮南去过浔阳。
牛渚由来险马当。
横江欲渡风波恶。
一水牵愁万里长。

No. 2

The sea tide surges south past Bankshine Town;
Mt. Ox Shoal is faced with Dangerous Horse.
The ferry throws gulping waves up and down;
My sad flow is a ten thousand mile course.

* Bankshine Town: an ancient name of modern-day Chiuchiang, Chianghsi Province.
* Mt. Ox Shoal: in today's Anhui Province, a place of military significance.
* Dangerous Horse: a mountain located in the lower reaches of the Yangtze River.

其 三

横江西望阻西秦，
汉水东连杨子津。
白浪如山哪可渡？
狂风愁杀峭帆人。

No. 3

Upstream I look: West Ch'in is barred from here;
The Han River links with Yangtze Ford there.
The waves are like mountains, how can we go?
The rough wind deals the helmsman a dead blow.

* the Han River: the longest branch of the Long River, having an important position in Chinese history.
* Yangtze Ford: located in the lower reaches of the Yangtze River.

其 四

海神来过恶风回，
浪打天门石壁开。
浙江八月何如此，
涛似连山喷雪来。

No. 4

Sea Demon gone, the evil wind comes on;
Waves break the stone wall and strike Heaven Gate.
Is the Ch'ient'ang River so the eighth moon,
Throwing up snow billows like mountains great?

* Heaven Gate: referring to Mt. Heaven Gate or Mt. Sky Gate.
* the Ch'ient'ang River: the lower reach of the Richspring River in present-day Hangchow, Chechiang Province.

其 五

横江馆前津吏迎，
向余东指海云生。
郎今欲渡缘何事，
如此风波不可行。

No. 5

Before the post the ferryman greets me;
He points to the dark clouds o'er the sea;
"Young man, why do you ferry just today?
Such wind and waves, you can't go anyway."

* ferryman: an official clerk managing boats at a ferry. Four to eight ferrymen were appointed at a ferry according to its size in the T'ang dynasty.

其 六

月晕天风雾不开，
海鲸东蹙百川回。
惊波一起三山动，
公无渡河归去来。

No. 6

The moon blurred by wind, the mist does not break;
The whale turning east, all rivers back flow.
The scaring waves rise and Three Mountains quake;
You will not come back if you try to row.

* the moon: the planet of the earth, which appears at night and gives off shining silvery light, an image of purity and solitude in Chinese culture.
* whale: a cetaceous mammal of fish-like form, especially one of the larger pelagic species, as distinguished from dolphins and porpoises. Whales have the fore limbs developed as broad flattened paddles, hind limbs absent, and a thick layer of fat or blubber immediately beneath the skin. A whale is a symbol of great ambition, fortitude and uniqueness.
* Three Mountains: There are three mountains overlooking the Yangtze River six kilometers north of Rivercalm County, that is, today's Nanking.

金陵城西楼月下吟

金陵夜寂凉风发，
独上高楼望吴越。
白云映水摇空城，
白露垂珠滴秋月。
月下沉吟久不归，
古来相接眼中稀。
解道澄江静如练，
令人长忆谢玄晖。

Crooning on Moonlit West Tower in Gold Hill Town

Night quiet, a chill blows across the Gold Hills；
I gaze afar into South Land upstairs.
The clouds in water shake the vacant town；
Lit by the autumn moon, the cold dew glares.
I croon for so long under the pale moon；
As e'er, talents are many, friends are few.
Thinking of his song: The calm river's white,
I admire his flair and his name Great Hue.

* the Gold Hills: the hills at Nanking.
* South Land: referring to where the states Wu and Yüeh were located, that is, the lower reaches of the Yangtze River.
* the moon: the celestial body that revolves around the earth from west to east as a satellite, which appears at night and gives off shining silvery light, an image of purity

and solitude in Chinese culture.
* Great Hue: referring to T'iao Hsieh (A.D. 464 – A.D. 499), an outstanding topographical poet in the Northern and Southern dynasties.

东 山 吟

携妓东山去，
怅然悲谢安。
我妓今朝如花月，
他妓古坟荒草寒。
白鸡梦后三百岁，
洒酒浇君同所欢。
酣来自作青海舞，
秋风吹落紫绮冠。
彼亦一时，此亦一时，
浩浩洪流之咏何必奇？

A Song of the East Hills

With a belle, I climb the East Hills;
At Hsieh's grave with gloom my soul fills.
My courtesan today is like a bloom;
His courtesan is decayed in his tomb.
Your dream of White Cock lasts three hundred years;
Wine sprinkled to you, let's drink up our cheers.
I compose a dance for you, drunk like that;
The autumn wind blows off my purple hat.
You were happy then, I am happy now;
It's no puzzle, our song the vast ocean does plough.

* the East Hills: the hills where An Hsieh (A.D. 320 – A.D. 385), a statesman and litterateur with high reputation, lived with ease and kept declining official positions

until he was in his forties. It is often used as a metaphor for a hermitage.

* dream of White Cock: an allusion to An Hsieh. At the age of sixty-six, An Hsieh dreamt that he got in the cart of his former commander, and the cart ran eight kilometers before they met a white cock. An Hsieh thought it was a symbol of an end of his sixteen years' official career, and the white cock was an ill omen according to his astrological analysis. As he thought, he passed away not long after. Since then, a White Cock dream has been used to indicate a bad omen.

* the vast ocean: an allusion to An Hsieh. Once Huan Wen, a minister in power in the Chin dynasty, wanted to kill An Hsieh in the meeting, Hsieh calmly recited a song of *Vast Ocean* and defused the crisis with his wisdom and broad mind.

僧　伽　歌

真僧法号号僧伽，
有时与我论三车。
问言诵咒几千遍，
口道恒河沙复沙。
此僧本住南天竺，
为法头陀来此国。
戒得长天秋月明，
心如世上青莲色。
意清净，貌棱棱。
亦不减，亦不增。
瓶里千年铁柱骨，
手中万岁胡孙藤。
嗟予落魄江淮久，
罕遇真僧说空有。
一言散尽波罗夷，
再礼浑除犯轻垢。

A Song of a Monk

O great monk, your Buddhist name is just monk;
Once you talked about three carts, o so grand.
One may croon and chant for a million times;
What one says is the Ganges, sand on sand.
Southern India's where you used to abide;
You came to this country Wisdom to impart.
You have attained the state of Real Moon Bright,

Like a green lotus living on one's heart.
A heart purified, a look sanctified.
With nothing decreased, with nothing increased.
An age-old relic in your gold vase grand,
An ancient rattan stick for your sage hand.
On the Huai I have for long roamed about;
No monk to tell me what's void, in or out.
While you croon, my Parajika's all gone
By another scripture, my sin's undone.

* three carts: In Buddhist concept, there are three carts—Ox Cart, Deer Cart, and Goat Cart, representing three different schools of Buddhism. Ox Cart indicates universal salvation of Mahayana for it can carry many lives; Deer Cart cannot carry as many as Ox Cart does; Goat Cart, with little strength, indicates self-salvation of Hinayana.
* the Ganges: the Indian Ganges River, often claimed as one of the greatest rivers in the world. Over 2,510 kilometers long, the Ganges originates high in the Himalayas where it makes its long and winding journey over India's greatest plain before draining into the Sunderban Delta and its final destination, the Bay of Bengal.
* the state of Real Moon Bright: a mental state that is clear and bright.
* lotus: one of the various plants of the waterlily family, characterized by their large floating round leaves and showy flowers, especially the white or pink Asian lotus, used as a religious symbol in Hinduism and Buddhism. In Chinese culture, it is a symbol of purity and elegance, unsoiled though out of soil, so clean with all leaves green, is a common image in Chinese literature, as two lines of a lyric by Hsiu Ouyang (A.D. 1007–A.D. 1072) read:"A thunder brings rain to the wood and pool, / The rain hushes the lotus, drips cool."
* with nothing decreased, with nothing increased: According to the Heart Sutra, "All Dharmas are empty of characteristics. They are not produced, not destroyed, not defiled, not pure; and they neither increase nor diminish."
* rattan: the long, tough, and flexible stem of a palm (genera Calamus and Daemonorops) growing in Asia, Africa and Australia, which can be used as material for the making of chairs and a variety of other furniture.
* the Huai: the Huai River, one of the seven rivers in China, between the Long River and the Yellow River, 1,000 kilometers long.
* Parajika: a Buddhist term, referring to capital felonies according to Buddhist discipline.

白云歌送刘十六归山

楚山秦山皆白云，
白云处处长随君。
长随君，君入楚山里，
云亦随君渡湘水。
湘水上，女萝衣，
白云堪卧君早归。

A Song of White Clouds to Liu Sixteen

White clouds drift o'er Mt. Ch'u and o'er Mt. Ch'in,
White clouds with you, here and there, out or in.
Here and there, out or in, they are with you in Ch'u's hills,
They are with you when you cross Hsiang's rills.
Crossing Hsiang's rills, pineapple clothes you don;
Come back soon, the white clouds you can lie on.

* Mt. Ch'u: Mt. Chaste, a representative of the mountains in Ch'u.
* Mt. Ch'in: any of the mountains in Ch'in.
* Hsiang: Three Hsiangs in full name, referring to modern-day Hunan Province.

金陵歌送别范宣

石头巉岩如虎踞，
凌波欲过沧江去。
钟山龙盘走势来，
秀色横分历阳树。
四十馀帝三百秋，
功名事迹随东流。
白马金鞍谁家子，
吹唇虎啸凤凰楼。
金陵昔时何壮哉！
席卷英豪天下来。
冠盖散为烟雾尽，
金舆玉座成寒灰。
扣剑悲吟空咄嗟，
梁陈白骨乱如麻。
天子龙沉景阳井，
谁歌玉树后庭花。
此地伤心不能道，
目下离离长春草。
送尔长江万里心，
他年来访南山皓。

A Song of the Gold Hills, Farewell to Hsuan Fan

Mt. Stone rugged like a tiger does crouch,
Seeming to jump o'er the Blue River, ouch!

Mt. Bell rolling like a dragon does coil,
The greenness stretches to paint Leeshine's soil.
More than forty reigns and three hundred years;
The river washes off all lords and peers.
Who is that young man riding a horse white?
He roars, climbing Phoenix Tower flight by flight.
How magnificent the Gold Hills of yore!
All heroes in the world come like a pour.
Now their crowns vanish, by wind blown away;
And their carts and sedans fall to decay.
Sword handle held in hand, long, long I sigh;
As dynasties rise and fall, white bones lie.
The emperor in Shadow Shine Well did cower;
Who will, as e'er, sing *Jade Tree Backyard Flower*?
One feels heart-stricken at this site, alas;
Now it runs rampant with luxuriant grass.
My heart will follow while upstream you row;
Next year, in the South Hills I will see you.

* Mt. Stone: an attraction with many relics, located in Gold Hill, i.e. today's Nanking, the capital of Chiangsu Province.
* Mt. Bell: located in the east of Gold Hill, today's Nanking.
* dragon: a fabulous serpent-like giant winged animal, a symbol of benevolence and sovereignty in Chinese culture.
* Leeshine: an ancient town of strategic importance, in present-day Ho County, Anhui Province. It is the hub of roads and waterways between the Long River and the Huai River, with a rich historic legacy such as Soul Shrine of Overlord Yü Hsiang, Yün Wu's Lane, Yarn Washer's Shrine and so on.
* That young man riding a horse white: implying Ching Hou (A.D. 503 - A.D. 552), a traitorous commander, who laid siege to Emperor of Liang's tower.
* The emperor in Shadow Shine Well: referring to Shupao Ch'en (A.D. 553 - A.D. 604), a king of Ch'en, who drowned himself in Shadow Shine Well to avoid being captured.
* *Jade Tree Backyard Flower*: a frivolous song composed by Shupao Ch'en, which is

regarded as a song of a fallen state.
* the South Hills: referring to Mt. Shang, famous for the four Wordist hermits, Ping T'ang, Kuang Ts'ui, Shih Wu and Shu Chou, who were invited as Highsire of Han's think tank in the early years of Han.

笑歌行

笑矣乎,笑矣乎。
君不见曲如钩,
古人知尔封公侯。
君不见直如弦,
古人知尔死道边。
张仪所以只掉三寸舌,
苏秦所以不垦二顷田。
笑矣乎,笑矣乎。
君不见沧浪老人歌一曲,
还道沧浪濯吾足。
平生不解谋此身,
虚作离骚遣人读。
笑矣乎,笑矣乎。
赵有豫让楚屈平,
卖身买得千年名。
巢由洗耳有何益,
夷齐饿死终无成。
君爱身后名,
我爱眼前酒。
饮酒眼前乐,
虚名何处有。
男儿穷通当有时,
曲腰向君君不知。
猛虎不看几上肉,
洪炉不铸囊中锥。
笑矣乎,笑矣乎。
宁武子,朱买臣,

扣角行歌背负薪。
今日逢君君不识，
岂得不如伴狂人。

Laughing and Singing

What a funny look; what a funny look!
Don't you see the bend is like a hook,
Ancients know that you can be a duke.
Don't you see the line is like a bow;
Ancients see that you will die so low.
That's why Ee Chang displayed his eloquent tongue;
That's why Ch'in Su wouldn't be a farming son.
What a funny look; what a funny look.
Don't you see the old man by the river sang a song,
And he could wash with water flowing on?
Yüan Ch'ü didn't know how to save himself;
He wrote verse for others' reading or shelf.
What a funny look; what a funny look.
In Chao was Yüjang, and in Ch'u Yüan Ch'ü;
They sold themselves to buy a name in vain.
Freedom washed up his ears to no avail;
Bow and Straight starved themselves only to fail.
You love your afterlife name fine;
I love my present mellow wine.
Present wine can offer you glee;
Nothingness a vain name can be.
A true hero goes with time and tide now;
A king knows nothing if to him you bow.
A tiger ignores the tabletop meat;

A furnace does not for an awl waste heat.
What a funny look; what a funny look.
Sir Mars Ning, Maich'en Chu, don't you tarry;
Why sing like that and why firewood carry?
If I meet you now but you don't know me,
Aren't you playing mad, a blockhead to be?

* Ee Chang: Ee Chang (? -309 B.C.), a political strategist and diplomat in the Warring States period, who gained his fame by outstanding eloquence and lobbying.
* Ch'in Su wouldn't be a farming son: Ch'in Su (? -284 B.C.), a political strategist in the Warring States period. When he succeeded, it occurred to him that if he had a farmland at an early age, he would not have been a prime minister.
* Yüan Ch'ü: Yüan Ch'ü (340 B.C.-278 B.C.), a great patriotic poet and official of Ch'u, the archetype of the incorruptible and faithful minister, repeatedly wronged by the king. His suicide at last by drowning in the Milo River is still commemorated every year throughout China by the Dragon Boat Festival.
* Yüjang: an assassin who wanted to take revenge for his master by killing Hsiangtsu Chao. He was captured after three failures. Knowing there would be no chance anymore, he asked Chao to let him stab his robe as if he had completed his mission. Chao agreed, and the assassin cut himself after thrusting three stabs on the latter's robe.
* Freedom: referring to Yu Hsu, a hermit of talent. He washed his ears as soon as he heard that Mound intended to abdicate his throne to him.
* Bow and Straight: referring to Bowone and Straightthree, childes in the late Shang dynasty. As they failed to admonish King Martial of Chough, they left King Chough and refused to take crops reaped under the reign of Chough. They lived on fungi on Mt. Firstshine and starved to death in the end.
* nothingness: a state of non-existence. Both Wordism and Christianity propagate the doctrine of the very beginning of the universe as nothing, out of which all were generated, that is, *ex nihilo*. Nothingness is also practiced in meditation, and even in governance in Wordism.
* a tiger: implying oppressive government.
* Sir Mars Ning: a posthumous title of Ch'i Ning, a meritorious statesman of Ch'i in the Spring and Autumn period. In his early age, Ning was poor and had no access to officialdom. When Lord Column of Ch'i passed by, Ning knocked on an ox horn and

sang out his frustration and attracted the lord's attention.
* Maich'en Chu: Maich'en Chu (? - 116 B.C.), a senior official, one of the nine powerful ministers in the Han dynasty. He was once a woodcutter, whose wife left him because of their poverty. By diligent study, however, he became prefect of K'uaichi; and his wife, who had sunk to destitution, begged to be allowed to rejoin him. But he replied, "If you can pick up spilt water, you may return; whereupon his wife went and hanged herself."

悲　歌　行

悲来乎，
悲来乎。
主人有酒且莫斟，
听我一曲悲来吟。
悲来不吟还不笑，
天下无人知我心。
君有数斗酒，
我有三尺琴。
琴鸣酒乐两相得，
一杯不啻千钧金。
悲来乎，悲来乎。
天虽长，地虽久，
金玉满堂应不守。
富贵百年能几何，
死生一度人皆有。
孤猿坐啼坟上月，
且须一尽杯中酒。
悲来乎，悲来乎。
凤凰不至河无图，
微子去之箕子奴。
汉帝不忆李将军，
楚王放却屈大夫。
悲来乎，悲来乎。
秦家李斯早追悔，
虚名拨向身之外。
范子何曾爱五湖，
功成名遂身自退。

剑是一夫用，
书能知姓名。
惠施不肯千万乘，
卜式未必穷一经。
还须黑头取方伯，
莫谩白首为儒生。

A Sad Song

Sad I am! So sad; Sad I am! So sad.
Wine if you have, don't fill your cup with wine;
Listen to me, a sad song I will whine.
When sad, if you don't sing or laugh with glee,
Then nobody in the world does know me.
You have a few barrels of wine;
I have a three-feet lute, lute mine.
A lute tune and wine, our pleasure twofold,
A cupful outdoes a jarful of gold.
Sad I am! So sad; sad I am! So sad.
The sky does roll vast; the earth does long last.
A houseful of treasures will vanish fast.
If one can live a hundred years, so what?
From life to death, everyone has the lot.
On the tomb wolves and foxes sit and whine;
Do cheer up and finish your cup of wine.
Sad I am! So sad; Sad I am! So sad.
If Phoenix did not light, there'd be no map;
Weitzu fled and Chitzu had his mishap.
Lord Martial did not treat General Li well;
King of Ch'u did Senior Yüan Ch'ü expel.

Sad I am! So sad; Sad I am! So sad.
If Ssu Li did come to regret that day,
He would all his vain honors throw away.
Li Fan to the nature did have access;
So he withdrew to lakes upon success.
A sword is just for one man's game;
A book you read to know your name.
Shi Hui did choose to reject a large state;
Shi Pu failed to finish a book deemed great.
You had better do something while in prime;
Do not be a scholar to waste your time.

* Weitzu: a brother of King Chow of Shang. Disappointed with the king's endless desires, he left the king.
* Chitzu: an uncle of King Chow of Shang. Failing to admonish the king, he pretended to be mad and was kept in captivity as a slave.
* General Li: Broad Li (? - 119 B.C.), Kuang Li if transliterated, a renowned general fighting against the Huns in the Han dynasty, called Flying General by the Huns.
* Yüan Ch'ü: Yüan Ch'ü (340 B.C.- 278 B.C.), a great patriotic poet and official of Ch'u, who threw himself into a river, so aggrieved at his broken state.
* Ssu Li: Ssu Li (284 B.C. - 208 B.C.), a renowned statesman, litterateur and calligrapher, whose political ideas has had a profound impact on China and laid the foundation of China's political system for more than two thousand years. After Emperor First of Ch'in died, Ssu was given a death penalty due to a false accusation. Before the execution, he sighed to his son that it would be impossible to hunt with his yellow dog anymore.
* Li Fan: Li Fan (536 B.C.- 448 B.C.), a renowned statesman, strategist, economist and Wordist in the Spring and Autumn period. Fan changed his name to live in seclusion after he helped State of Yüeh wipe out Wu.
* Shi Hui: Shi Hui (390 B.C. - 317 B.C.), a nominalist philosopher, statesman and strategist in the Warring States period, and one of Sir Lush's closest friend. He was one of the proponents of "vertical union" against the "horizontal alliance" supporting Ch'in.

* Shi Pu: an official in the Western Han dynasty. An illiterate shepherd in his early age, he sponsored the Han court during the fight against the Huns, and was appointed as a senior official afterwards.